IN TERROR'S DEADLY CLASP

A Novel
Based on a True
9/11 Story

JILL AMADIO

Library of Congress Cataloging-in-Publication Data

Copyright 2021 Jill Amadio

ISBN 978-1-7326560-9-3

Cover design by Karen Phillips/PhillipsCovers.com

Dedication

"In Terror's Deadly Clasp" is a story-within-a-story and is dedicated to the woman who trusted the author to publish a fictionalized account of her life.

Too many pay a price for coming forward in order to provide assistance, share their experiences for the good of all, and to clear their conscience. Sometimes such people are tricked into believing that a whistleblower can be fully protected and safe from revenge or simply to avoid an inconvenient truth being made public.

Many whistleblowers are scorned for revealing what they know and for exposing warning signs as was Sofia Wainwright, the young woman who inspired this work and whose real name must be kept secret.

The novel is also dedicated to those who died as a result of the September 11, 2001 attacks on the United States of America not only on that fateful day but in the days, months, and years to come.

What dread grasp
Dare its deadly terrors clasp?

Tyger! Tyger!
William Blake
1757-1827

Chapter 1

"Oh, my God. It really is him!"

Hunched over the front page of the local Sun-Star newspaper spread out on the built-in beige Formica table, Sofia Wainwright Jarrett stared intently at the images of the nineteen 9/11 hijackers. Fear swept through her like a tide of molten lava.

She sat alone in the double-wide trailer she shared with Preston Jarrett, her second husband, and their three children in the gritty little city of Felicidad, Northern California. The panic that set her heart pounding, after her brother Jeff Wainwright's phone call an hour earlier to the Angus Grill restaurant where she waitressed, returned in full force.

As she studied the hijackers' photos and identities released to the media by the Federal Bureau of Investigation days after the attack on the World Trade Center in New York City one narrow, dark face instantly captured her attention. It was that of her first husband whom the Bureau identified as Aswad al-Lufti although she knew him by another name, Karim ibn Riyad.

1

There must be a mistake. Sofia's hands trembled as she smoothed out the newspaper page again and again. There was Karim and, farther along in the same row, head shots of his two brothers, Nafir and Hassan, their images staring straight at her. She remembered them as 20-something Arab students. How could they be among the 9/11 terrorists? They danced in nightclubs, hired hookers, binged on burgers and pizzas, and dabbed expensive colognes on their faces. They loved the Western lifestyle and were intoxicated with its freedoms. They were like kids released from class indulging in forbidden smoking and drinking. With the terrible attacks of September 11, 2001 when had the young men she knew become angry murderers?

She looked again at the faces in the newspaper. No, there was no mistake. Her brother was right. She'd know that weaselly face of her ex-husband anywhere. Memories of the many Middle Eastern men who were almost daily visitors to her home also swam into her consciousness. She had spent three years with them. They'd ignored her most of the time but that was their way with women, Karim told her. It meant nothing.

Why didn't the FBI believe me in 1993, she thought, her fear at realizing her situation quickly replaced by fury. Why hadn't they trusted my warnings when I told them that I was sure terrorist sleeper cells were being organized in my home? That I watched the Arab students take flying lessons, and photograph landmark buildings? She remembered telling the Special Agents at the local FBI field office that she suspected the men were plotting something dangerous. However, the information that Sofia brought to the FBI in both Portland and San Diego was of no interest to the bureau. Sofia also went to the San Diego District Attorney's offices. Again, she was rebuffed, failing to produce any curiosity about the sleeper cell activities to which she was privy for two years.

She was regarded with obvious skepticism over her warnings of a potential terrorist conspiracy. The agents scoffed at the descriptions of the young Arab students' activities in the Pacific Northwest, of Sofia being present at recruitment meetings, secret sleeper cell gatherings, weekly reconnaissance operations, target-planning discussions where she often heard the name Osama bin Laden, and the ordnance maps they scrutinized and squabbled over. The FBI sent Sofia home with a sharp rebuke about an overactive imagination.

On February 26, 1993, three weeks after her visit to the FBI, the parking garage and basement beneath the World Trade Center in New York were bombed. Was it a precursor to future attacks? Had the terrorists planned to demolish the Twin Towers from below, and, failing to do so, plotted the next attack to strike from above?

The report that Sofia read in the newspaper days after 9/11 claimed that Karim was identified as Hijacker Number 13 on United Airlines Flight 175 that crashed into the South Tower of the World Trade Center. Now, still reeling from the page in front of her she chewed on her bottom lip and studied the other hijackers' faces. Dear God. She recognized two others, then three more. She knew six of the terrorists, two of them intimately. They were her former brothers-in-law.

Or were they?

Chapter 2

"Sofia! Have you seen the news?"

It was barely an hour since she heard the hysteria in Jeff's voice as he shouted into the phone on the reservation desk at the Angus Grill. His call initially brought a smile to Sofia's lips. She was used to the pranks her brother played on the family and today seemed to be no exception but when the manager told her to keep it brief she was annoyed with Jeff. As the two youngest of the six Wainwright siblings, Sofia and Jeff were close and in childhood often played tricks on each other. This time, however, it was a poor choice of timing.

"What news? Stop with the jokes. You know better than to call me here, Jeff. I love you, kid, but you'll get me fired. Call me later at home. My shift has three more hours to go. How's it going at the warehouse? No, don't tell me. I have to hang up."

Sofia had been working for only for five weeks. With unemployment at thirteen percent in the area she was not about to jeopardize her job at the best steak house in Felicidad. She brought in good tips, some of the highest among the wait staff, with her smile and friendly manner.

It was the end of summer; George W. Bush was eight months into his presidency, and barely three weeks earlier the U.S. Government lost track of $2.3 billion in Pentagon funds. But that amount of money held no meaning for Sofia.

"Go home right now!" Jeff's voice became louder and more frenzied amid the clatter of plates and noisy diners around her. "Look at the TV, damn it. Go buy the newspaper. It's Karim. He's on the front page. He was one of the 9/11 hijackers although the FBI says his name was something different. But it's him, I'm telling you, sis. His brothers and buddies are there, too, the ones Mom and I met at your house on the river. It's them. Call me back when you've seen the photos."

Stunned, Sofia stood still, unbelieving. She'd never heard her brother so upset. He sounded frightened. Karim was one of the 9/11 hijackers? Sofia hung up the phone, went over to the cash register to tell the restaurant manager's wife she had an urgent, personal emergency and needed to leave right away.

"Your face has turned white, Sofia. Anything I can do?"

"Thanks, but no. I'm so sorry. Maybe it will turn out not to be anything much after all but I have to check it out."

Her brother's words about her ex-husband's involvement in the 9/11 attacks several days earlier were so outside her realm of reality that her mind almost shut down. Was it true? It was all she could do to drive the fifteen minutes it took to reach their trailer after stopping briefly at the Circle K convenience store to buy the newspaper, fumbling for coins in her waitress apron pocket. Without looking at the paper she stuffed it into her purse, got back into her small Honda, and drove home.

Sofia had finally been able to put her teenage marriage and divorce behind her although when she and Karim parted she felt as if her heart had split into pieces. She'd wept for days and felt the pain physically affecting her. He was her first at the age of 17 and she'd fallen for him fiercely and unconditionally, estranging herself at times from her family.

Five years after their 1994 divorce Sofia started a new life in Felicidad with Jarrett, a straightforward, kindly man who worked as a farm hand. It wasn't much of a job but with her wages and tips from the steak house added to the pot, they managed. Their two babies, born little more than a year apart, were happy little boys. Sofia also had a six-year old son, Cody, from an earlier, short-lived relationship.

In this part of California, the Central Valley where agricultural grasslands were a mainstay, there wasn't a lot of excitement to start the tumbleweeds rolling. Some of the residents lived on small-time drug dealing and growing marijuana, unlawful at the time, while others worked the fields of crops that were legal and back-breaking.

Felicidad, settled by Germans in 1872, occupied just over five square miles and was barely a stopover for folks looking for a gas station along state highway 77. The majority of residents were ranch hands and migratory workers, most of whom had never left after arriving for seasonal work in the surrounding area. Six miles to the east was the city of Merced, the county seat, popular for its nearby fishing and water sports. Thirty miles north was Modesto, the home of Chandra Levy and Laci Peterson who would become murder victims a year after 9/11. Two hours' drive north was the state capital of Sacramento, and to the east was Yosemite National Park.

To Sofia, Felicidad offered the kind of ordinary, normal life she'd been seeking. She welcomed its bland anonymity. Here, she felt safe, hidden, the past locked away. She had lived through enough chaotic and bewildering traumas to last a few lifetimes until finding sanctuary with Jarrett. Knowing herself tougher and wiser, her only wish was to be the core of their young family.

But now her past was back delivering a knockout punch. The grief she had shed like a second skin years ago was threatening to clothe her again. She re-lived in her mind as if in a nightmare the events of 9/11 as she watched it repeatedly unfolding on television as the terrifying events followed one after the other, the unforgiving lethal steel-winged arrows of death piercing high up into the Twin Towers of the World Trade Center. She imagined her ex-husband racing up and down the aisle of United Airlines Flight 175 that slammed into the South Tower between floors 77 and 85. She could see Karim's bony arms propelling him forward as he boarded the United Airlines plane, those scrawny legs shaking with excitement. He'd be pumped all right, she thought sourly.

Sofia stared so hard at the newspaper photo on the table that had her eyes been daggers they would have pierced it. She threw it down in disgust and went out to her car. The little Honda Accord hatchback always felt to her like a protective cocoon. It was second-hand, twelve years old and not worth squat but she kept it as shiny as if it were a Rolls-Royce. The car was a far cry from the large Mercedes-Benz and Lincoln sedans she rode around in with Karim and his Arab friends. As she sat in the driver's seat thinking through the implications and consequences of her previous marriage she had thought was buried in the past, she felt dizzy.

Yes, she realized she had indeed been part of some of the 9/11 hijackers' lives. And yes, those deceiving murderers, especially Karim, had manipulated her teenage gullibility so cleverly. Had she accepted it all back then because they were fascinating foreigners and her need for a man to love her was so strong before he turned on her? How dumb she'd been. She'd carried the wound of Karim's rejection for two years until she was finally able to bury him from her mind and stop thinking of herself as his dependent victim.

Now, it all threatened to come rushing back.

Chapter 3

Sofia changed channels every three seconds on the small television set sitting on a metal stand. The hijackers' photos still stared out from each news station along with shots of the burning, collapsing towers and of the two other attacks, all terrible images that would play for months and years into the future.

It's not possible, thought Sofia. Her ex-husband was just a skinny young student born in the United Arab Emirates, a country she'd never heard of, and then he had gone with his family to live in Saudi Arabia. Today's newspaper story, under banner headlines, reported that he and his brothers, Zafir and Hassan, were aboard United Airlines Flight 175 and that one of Karim's cousins was on United Airlines Flight 93 that crashed into a field in Shanksville, in rural Pennsylvania. The newspaper gave all three relatives different first and last names from those she knew them by.

She remembered talking on the phone to Karim's parents in Saudi Arabia several times when she was living with him and often after they were married. She enjoyed the conversations with her father-in-law, Bathshar, and mother-in-law, Saidah, whenever they spoke although Saidah spoke little English. Was Karim's dad part of the 9/11 plot?

Back in the trailer Sofia leaned into the small bedroom closet and pulled down a shoebox from the top shelf. She was looking for the only photograph she kept of Karim. She'd thrown out their wedding photos when she married Prescott Jarrett.

"It can't be true," Sofia mumbled.

She grabbed the magnifying glass from the kitchen drawer. The Sun-Star's grainy image of him loomed large as she focused centimeter by centimeter on the man's deep-set, hypnotic slate-black eyes so dark and impenetrable the irises and pupils blended together like a pair of black marbles. She remembered her first date with him, startled by their intensity. She studied the high forehead where his hairline receded, the long chin, and his full lips. Sofia grasped at straws to pretend it wasn't really him.

"Karim's nose was larger. His cheeks were fatter," she said out loud.

But she knew she was fooling herself. She was familiar with every inch of Karim ibn Riyad's face and had never forgotten a single feature. Using the magnifying glass again she compared the newspaper picture with the photo taken many years earlier and banished to the shoebox. He was photographed sitting in McDonald's where her sister, Anne, worked, a large order of French fries between his hands. Sofia remembered how he devoured hamburgers, pizza and other fast food like a starving wolf and never put on a pound. She had snapped his picture with her instant throwaway Kodak camera as he sat opposite her in the booth grinning ear-to-ear, overdressed as usual in a white silk suit, a black shirt, and a black tie.

She always got a kick out of Karim's fake bad-guy look. He liked to wear gangster-style clothes like the Mafia and carried around a Marksman 1010 in his waistband. It was only a BB gun but it looked like the real McCoy. He'd load and unload it constantly, filling the chamber with pellets or bolts. Guns were nothing new to Sofia. Hunters looking for deer and elk were regular visitors to her home state of Oregon. Although her religion forbade guns her brothers often found rusty old BB rifles in the woods. With no money to spend on pellets the boys scoured junk yards looking for ball bearings. The Marksman was the only weapon Sofia saw Karim handle, she remembered, telling him it was really a kid's toy but she could see he thought of himself as a Cosa Nostra soldier with it. She always laughed at him.

As her gaze again swept over the newspaper images of the 19 hijackers, at the television scenes of the two towers collapsing, she acknowledged that her former husband along with his fellow hijackers had commandeered a different, more deadly weapon than a BB gun, one that was unprecedented, and killed thousands of Americans on a cloudless morning in September.

Sofia continued to compare her photo of her former husband to the one in the newspaper. She no longer doubted the hijacker was him. Neither, she found out when they phoned, did her brothers Frank and Alan and her sister Heather. Most convinced of all the siblings that hijacker #13 was definitely Karim was Anne. It was she who had introduced him to Sofia in 1992 and had last seen him in 1994.

Chapter 4

With fury turning back to fear and overtaking her like a tsunami Sofia returned her brother's phone call.

"Jeff, I'm home," she said, still trembling as she heard him pick up. "I have his photo in the newspaper and he's on TV."

"It is him, isn't it?"

"Damn right." She could barely get the words out her throat was so tight. "My brain's gone haywire. How did I end up with a terrorist?"

"I'd never have believed it either if I hadn't seen the news."

"Was I really such a stupid kid back then? How could I have been in love with that pathetic little man?"

"Sofia, you were one of the smartest students in school. Of course you're not stupid. Blinded by love, it looks like you just hooked up with a madman, that's all. Yeah, I admit that Mom and some of us thought you were real naïve. But Mom said you were so impulsive and rebellious you wouldn't have listened to her anyway."

"Jeff, I have to do something about this."

"No, no you don't." He sounded agitated again. "Now look, don't go off the rails here. Don't do anything rash. You just need to be aware of what's what, that's all. We all need to lay low. Don't tell anything to anyone."

"Easy for you to say." She managed a weak laugh but it died in her throat.

My God, she thought, more than 2,800 victims. She looked at the wall clock. Almost one-thirty. Her mother-in-law was babysitting Hank and Benjie and wasn't due back for another hour. Cody was still at school. Sofia spoke into the phone again.

"The newspaper article said that the FBI is asking anyone who has ever seen or has information about these guys should immediately contact their nearest office or call their hotline. I really should do that."

"No! Please, I strongly advise you not to, Sofia, You'll only stir things up for all of us and our families. They'll strip your life to the bone. You've got Prescott and the kids to think about."

"I know but if I can save just one person from another attack by speaking up about what I know of the 9/11 terrorists then I think I need to say something. Maybe I'll give the FBI in Sacramento a call."

"Look, do you want me to come there?" said Jeff. "I can take a few days off work."

"Sure. No. Oh, I don't know. I wish I knew what to do. I feel so ashamed."

"You did nothing wrong. It's not as if he was one of those poor old mangy stray dogs you used to rescue and care for. And remember all those feral cats you brought home? Sofia, you did nothing wrong. You just married the guy, that's all." He cut short a chuckle

"Thanks a lot, dear brother." She knew it was his way of trying to break the tension he hears in my voice, she thought.

"Doesn't make me feel any better either, Sofia, to know the creep was my brother-in-law. I can't think of anything more horrific than knowing he was one of the hijackers."

She glanced in the small mirror next to the refrigerator as she paced, the cordless phone pressed to her ear. The effects of the past hour showed in red splotches on her face, but the pale blond hair that Karim always liked her to wear long and loose was tied neatly in a ponytail and the eyes he once compared to blue sapphires from Persia were clouded with tears.

"Gotta go," she said, and hung up.

She felt paralyzed, frozen all over again. She recalled the passion she felt for her first husband, how deeply she loved him, how fascinated she was with everything he did and said until his behavior turned the marriage into a bitter battle and they divorced. Sofia was convinced he had fallen in love with someone else, or was having several affairs. Even then and for a couple of years afterwards she held out hope for a reconciliation and was willing to forgive his cheating with other women. Now, her brother was trying to avoid pointing out that she'd shared her bed with a mass murderer.

The phone rang. It was Sofia's mother, Erika, calling from the house of one of her other daughters, Heather, in South Carolina. They had both seen Erika's former son-in-law and his brothers' photos in Parade magazine. Beside herself with worry, frantic about her daughter's and grandchildren's safety, Erika had no doubt that hijacker #13 was Karim. Only Sofia's brother Ben was not totally convinced. However, much later, because of circumstances, he changed his mind.

"Hi, Mom. Thanks for calling." Sofia repressed a sob. "I guess this ruins your vacation down there. You know, I'm thinking of calling the FBI although they'll probably dismiss me like last time."

"Sofia, please don't tell anyone about Karim," Erika said. "It's scary. If you tell the FBI they can hurt you. Please lay low. You could be blacklisted by our own government. Or al Qaeda could find you."

"Mom, I am savvy enough to understand the consequences if I contact the authorities but I must. There could be more attacks. I may have a lot of information I can pass along. I knew those guys so well, their habits and culture."

"Honey, you are highly underestimating what can happen to you, your family, and all of us."

"I'm sorry. I have to do it," she said, tears falling as she hung up the phone.

It rang again immediately. It was Alan calling from Arizona.

"Guess you've seen the news, kid."

"My God, it's him, right? Mom and Jeff say it is, so do Heather and Anne. They're as horrified as I am."

"Sure looks like it's him. I only met him one time but his face stayed with me. I'm so sorry."

"Jeff and the others think I should lay low and say nothing but I think I should go to the FBI and tell them what I know. I ought to tell them that I met some of the others, too and I was in on their cell meetings and activities although I didn't understand much at the time. I cringe now to think how I welcomed them all with smiles. What do you think I should do?"

"Sofia, you have to say something, you just can't sit on it. If you can save people by what you tell the authorities then you need to contact them and tell them what you know. Perhaps there are more attacks in the works that other terrorists are plotting against our country. You had a personal insight into these jerks, and you should tell the FBI."

"I agree. We need to destroy these monsters. I'm not proud of my past, Alan, but I am proud to stand up and be counted. I still can't understand why I was so trusting with Karim, so believing."

"Just the way you were back then, kiddo."

19

Chapter 5

"Is this the ghostwriter?"

The woman's voice was hesitant, slightly breath-less. She sounded young. Mid-twenties, I guessed.

"Yes. This is Victoria McAuley."

I paused. Describing my qualifications wasn't necessary until I knew why the caller was phoning me. Some people just needed to find out what I did and how the process of ghostwriting worked. Others who wanted a full-blown explanation preferred to hear it in person rather than read it on my web site and a few, the elderly, didn't use computers.

"I need to write a book."

"What kind of book are you thinking of writing?" I asked.

"My name is Sofia Wainwright Jarrett and I want to tell my story. I was married to one of the 9/11 hijackers, Karim ibn Riyad. It will be a book about my life with him. A memoir."

Oh Lord, they're still coming out of the wood-work, I thought. The months following the bombing of the World Trade Center produced several foreign and American women who claimed to be wives or girlfriends of one or another of the 9/11 terrorists. One story of an Anaheim, California woman's marriage to a man she came to believe was a terrorist occurred in 1993 and was well-documented. She told an Orange County, California newspaper reporter that she had taken her suspicions to the FBI but was ignored. The same scenario as Sofia, I was later to learn. I turned my attention back to my caller.

"What evidence do you have to back up your story?"

"I worked with the FBI for ten months after I told them who I was and about my life with Karim. I have all the Special Agents' names who debriefed me and sent me to the bars and the places where Karim and I went to party and socialize with his Arab friends. I have his photo."

"Do you have anything to prove you were married to this hijacker?"

"Yep. I have my marriage certificate, the divorce decree, and some documents. I have information about my former in-laws who live in Saudi Arabia. You can talk to some of my family who met this scumbag I married, and I have other stuff."

This piqued my interest one hundred percent. But literary hoaxes claiming to be true were still fresh in the public's mind, such as James Frey's "A Million Little Pieces," a memoir that was proven to be fake. Nevertheless, I was between projects and the woman's statement stirred my investigative juices left over from my journalism days. Couldn't hurt to check it out.

"Why come forward now?" I asked.

"That's part of my story. It's taken me this long to come to terms with what happened and how it ripped my life apart not only on 9/11 but for almost a year afterwards. I have just finished working with federal law enforcement agents after telling them my story and being an undercover informant."

"Did you sign any document with them that prohibits you from going public?"

"No, nothing like that. After 9/11 I guess official contracts went by the board, they were so anxious to talk to people like me who knew these guys. I've gone back and forth on whether to find someone to write and publish my story or not. Most of all, my main motive to do a book is to alert others to what may seem normal but are actually red flags. My story isn't a rehashing of the 9/11 attacks. It's my personal experiences with the terrorists I knew. I was with some of them during the early planning stages."

"You could be ridiculed if no one believes you."

"The FBI believes me."

Chapter 6

Within a week I was driving to Oregon to meet a woman who claimed to have married a 9/11 hijacker. It sounded far-fetched. She said she had proof and provided names, places, and dates. Did I want to get involved in a project that could turn out to be a figment of someone's imagination, someone who wanted to be famous, or who craved attention? I'd worked with clients with these needs and they didn't bother me. I considered myself a literary advisor as well as a ghostwriter and of course their books were their own to fashion as they wished. However, I'd point out that if certain judgements were hurtful, revengeful, or unnecessary, their book would be better off without such comments.

I had no idea of Sofia's reason for wanting to write a book except, I supposed, to relieve her conscience, or to relate her experiences of living with a 9/11 hijacker and its consequences. I would need to find out if her story was true. She mentioned meeting several times for debriefing sessions with FBI Special Agents. She gave me their names and telephone numbers. That information swung the pendulum in her favor. I decided it was worth a shot. I packed a suitcase, filled up the car with gas, and on my way to the Interstate 5 stopped at the post office to fill out a Hold the Mail postcard.

The route north, a straight shot all the way on Interstate 5 from my home in Southern California to Dundee, Oregon where she was staying with her mother, would take about sixteen hours, I calculated. I enjoyed long drives alone and discovering views, places, and towns I never knew existed. I was often stunned by the natural beauty of every state I visited. America was a revelation to me, an ex-pat who missed Cornwall in the United Kingdom but embraced this vast, incredibly diverse country.

As I drove I gave more thought to my current mission of meeting up with a woman who claimed she was married to one of the 9/11 hijackers. Images of that terrible morning flooded into my consciousness as I, like millions, had seen the attacks unfold on television. We watched in disbelief as the second hijacked airliner smashed directly head-on into the South Tower of the World Trade Center.

The fire and smoke still belching from the first plane's unerring aim towards the North Tower and the subsequent collapse of both towers are forever imprinted on the minds of all those who witnessed the destruction and deaths of the almost 3,000 people who died. Conceived by Osama bin Laden in

1988 when he founded al Qaeda, which translates to "the base," the militant Islamist organization would blossom into a worldwide group with head-quarters in Afghanistan and become allied with the Taliban militia.

If Sofia was to be believed, that her ex-husband actually was on Flight 175, would she be safe after publishing the book she intended to write? Would I, as her ghostwriter? My name would not be on the book, of course, but usually clients thanked me by name on the Acknowledgements page. The wording was mostly simple and brief, "Thanks to Victoria McAuley for her help." I am still waiting for a client to write on their Acknowledgements page, "Thanks to Victoria McAuley for writing my entire book for me."

I forced all thoughts about Sofia and the hijacker from my mind for the moment and focused on the spectacular scenery along the way. I slowed down to enjoy the sight of snow-clad volcanic Mount Shasta, the fifth highest mountain in California. It dominated the landscape, rising abrupt and solitary close to the freeway. I made a mental note to stop by the little town that hugged its foothills, nine miles south, on my return trip if this hijacker project proved to be a hoax.

My research papers explained that Mount Shasta had erupted in 1786 and that the area was the oldest known settlement in America, going back 7,000 years. I was more interested in the town itself, though, as a spiritual center with metaphysical shops selling Shasta Indian products, crystals, wicca goblets, Chakra jewelry, and such. I'd once ghostwritten a book for a psychic and wondered if he'd foreseen the electronic age when, in 1992, the World-Wide Web was born, allowing everyone to communicate online. I wrote some business books, too, but most of my clients were elderly grandfathers and grandmothers who wanted their children to know about their heritage.

If this trip turned out to be a bust maybe I'd also stop on my way home at Mike and Tony's restaurant and enjoy their Happy Hour after I toured the Lake Shasta underground caverns that were situated 800 feet up the mountain. They were famous for their colorful columns, stalagmites and stalactites studded with crystals. As an archaeologist freak I watched any TV show that featured the ancient past.

I'd brought a tuna salad sandwich and a thermos of coffee to eat in the car so when I pulled off the road at a gas station, I ate lunch. Then I continued to travel past the turn-off for Yosemite National Park, another magnificent area I'd vowed to visit. When a sign for Grant's Pass showed up along the highway I thought about its fame as Oregon's capital for whitewater rafting along the Rogue River. It was tempting to look for an exit from the I-5 where I could pull off and watch for any brave souls battling its rough, swift-flowing waters. The Rogue was also renowned for world-class fishing but I was anxious to get to Dundee.

Another temptation to linger was at a group of eleven wineries including a champagne cellar south of the Interstate 5 at the Pass. Maybe I'd stop by a couple of them, too, on my way home. As I learned a day later when I was with Sofia's mother and she took me on a tour in and around Dundee, there were several additional wineries and champagne cellars west and south of town.

The state line between California and Oregon was coming up and after I crossed it I stopped in the nearest service plaza to celebrate with a coffee and a couple of cream donuts. I got back into my car with spirits high, looking forward to the last leg of my journey and meeting the young woman called Sofia Wainwright Jarrett, mulling over book titles in my mind and quickly dismissing the obvious, "I Married a 9/11 Hijacker," for something a little more intriguing. Sofia's story could be mistaken for a thriller from what I knew so far from our phone conversations.

I crested Grant's Pass, estimating I was only 70 miles or so from my destination. Having made good time I decided to stop in the city itself to inspect the 17-ft. tall Neanderthal caveman statue. I wanted to see it in person after finding photos in which he is wielding the ubiquitous caveman's club. His location, I read, was on a giant rock pedestal in an outdoor plaza. I needed to take a break and take a short walk to stretch my legs but when I arrived at the site the pedestal was unoccupied. The sculpture was missing. On inquiry I was told he was having graffiti removed from his fur-covered torso.

Once more on the highway I slipped the recently-released Donald Walters "Mystic Harp" CD into the player and reveled in listening to harpist Derek Bell's rendition of music in the Celtic tradition, much beloved when I was growing up in Cornwall. Driving into Oregon I sang along with the songs, remembering my mother's dancing school in St. Ives where she taught ballet, tap, and folk dancing.

However, the music and the brief stop failed to keep my mind off Sofia's story and I was pleased when, an hour and a half later, I reached the Dundee exit. I discovered that the Interstate 5 sliced partway through the west side of town. Surrounded by mountains to the east behind Crater Lake, the little town was founded in 1797 by a Scottish immigrant, Iain Dundee who saw incredible riches in the surrounding forests nestled in the Umpqua River Valley.

I couldn't resist checking out this settler online before I left home. I'd done the same when I visited Sedona, Arizona a couple of years earlier when ghost-writing a biography. That town was named for the postmaster's wife, Sedona, after the United States government declined the postmaster's two previous suggestions, declaring them too long. Really? I was reminded of the little village on the Isle of Anglesey in Wales that boasts the longest name in Europe. It has sixty-three letters, includes a triple "l," and translates to "St. Mary's Church in the hollow of the white hazel tree near a rapid whirlpool and the Church of St. Tysilio near the red cave."

As I drove through Dundee I pondered Iain Dundee's choice to cross the entire country before picking a place where he decided he could make a living. So many pioneers settled in the Great Plains states and some stopped traveling once they reached Mississippi. The wagon train stories are so rich in detail I imagined the Scot sitting upfront holding the reins and urging the horses on faster and faster.

Before I left home I'd consulted Wikipedia's website which as usual came up trumps and supplied the answer to why he kept going to the West Coast and Oregon. I learned that when he sailed from the British Isles, the Scottish forests where he worked as a lumberman had already been badly decimated to fill the needs of the burgeoning number of new factories and houses being built. Timber became a high-priced commodity.

In Oregon the Scot quickly saw a way to make his fortune felling and exporting back to England the natural resources all round him. Although New England, and Maine in particular, became the world's largest lumber shipping port, the Pacific Northwest would follow right behind.

With those facts in mind I wasn't in the least surprised to find that the first commercial establishment I saw after taking the Dundee exit was a motel built in the style of a log cabin. The office was the largest building and seven cabins stretched into the wilderness behind. Everything looked neat, clean, and inviting but when I asked the room prices they were far beyond my budget. For a change, I was taking on the writing of Sofia's story without a fee and I therefore needed to keep an eye on expenses usually covered by clients.

I continued on through town, passing railroad tracks and a tire center. Almost at the other end of Dundee, traversed in about 20 minutes, I spotted another motel near a shopping mall. This one looked more reasonably priced than the previous motel, which suited my depleted bank account. I registered and found myself in a dreary room that smelled of mold.

It was still light although late afternoon and time for a quick ride around town. I discovered that while the greatest wealth came from lumber, canneries and brickyards, there was a thriving boutique winery industry. The town of around 20,000 people was situated on lands previously owned by several Indian tribes including Cow Creek Band of the Umpqua. There were waterfalls nearby, and rivers for salmon, steelhead, bluegill, and trout.

I called Sofia, told her my room number, and arranged for us to meet the next morning. At the shopping mall I picked up some Chinese take-out for dinner and returned to my room. As I fell asleep under the musty blanket I wondered if I was on a wild goose-chase. It wouldn't be the first in my line of business but it sure promised to be the most fascinating if it was true. It also held the potential of proving I was one great big patsy.

Chapter 7

As soon as Sofia stepped through my open door and over the threshold the next morning it was as if a sunbeam had pierced the gloom. Her shoulder-length blonde hair gleamed like spun gold and a sweet smile radiated. The sun behind Sofia's silhouette bathed her in an eerie light and I felt her sense of anticipation.

She was luminescent, ablaze with energy and clearly eager and excited to meet me. What had I expected after hearing the main points of her story over the phone? A sorrowful woman, perhaps? A guilt-stricken neurotic? She was neither of these. Instead, I found myself faced with a stunning, model-slender dazzler. Although her smile revealed a slight overbite of her front teeth it couldn't diminish her beauty. But as I looked into her large, blue eyes framed by long lashes I saw a vulnerability, an uncertainty that I assumed was due to the events she'd briefly described by phone and would now be forcing herself to re-live.

I was worried we might not click or find a rapport. Ghostwriting depends greatly on being able to empathize with clients, to read their body language, learn their "voice" and patterns of speech. Above all, clients need a willingness to confide, secrets they had never told anyone else but wanted to express in a book for only the family to read and not commercially published or sold.

My concerns with this new client were unfounded. As Sofia drove us over to a diner for a late breakfast and an initial talk she chatted comfortably about her project, how she'd changed her mind about it a dozen times, worried about finding a simpatico biographer, and how pleased she was she'd called me after reading my resume on the Authors Guild website.

We found a booth in the back. The diner was almost empty for which I was grateful. I wanted to use the tape recorder and in public places any background noises often drowned out conversation. Thankfully, it was quiet where we were sitting at the other end of the door to the kitchen and to the front door.

After ordering coffee I labeled a cassette tape with her name and the date, numbered it and slipped it into my tape recorder. I pushed the Record and Play buttons, made sure it was turned up to its highest volume, and began listening to the story I'd driven to Oregon to hear.

"Sofia, how did you meet this terrorist? It sounds pretty far-fetched."

She grimaced. "It does, doesn't it? But it is all too real."

With anger, shame, and sadness alternately registering on her face, Sofia assured me that she was prepared to recount experiences to me that over the next weeks would be startling, shocking and almost unbelievable. For my part, I knew that if I believed her I'd be making several trips to Dundee before I was able to flesh out the story, create an outline, and write the book.

I also knew there'd be extensive research into the terrible event and attempts to interview law enforcement agencies. I had doubts about the FBI Special Agents agreeing to talk to me but Sofia's hundreds of pages of notes written down after each session with the FBI were compelling. She provided a depth of information that not only convinced me of the truth for which she was offering details but also because she knew I would check up on what she was claiming.

Usually when ghostwriting a book for a client who wants to reveal a painful period in their life or secrets they want to share in order to release themselves from perceived guilt, I research until the well is dry. For a World War II biography I perused thirty-four books before beginning to write about a certain part of it.

Some of my research for Sofia's project included books that were already published about 9/11, just months after it happened. But I wanted to delve more deeply, instead, into the personal side of these terrorists as they went about their everyday business here in America. I needed Sofia's insights into the dynamics of their daily lives, their behavior, and information about the college classes they claimed to be attending. I wanted to know if and how they blended into the background of America's culture. How did these terrorists or zealots, whatever they were, manage to stay under the radar for so long before putting their plans into action? I wanted to learn their habits, their likes and dislikes, facets of their personalities, and find out how they practiced their religion if, indeed, they did. I already knew that many of the hijackers were not students although they were welcomed into the U.S. on student visas. Even those who went to local colleges for a while soon discarded all pretense of attending class.

I realized I needed much more background of a general context than Sofia could provide. There were hundreds of articles analyzing the attacks and events that are reported to have led up to them. There were talking heads, analysts, experts, psychiatrists, and pundits on every radio and television station offering their views on the why and wherefores. Dozens of pompous U.S. Government officials took to the airwaves to expound on why and how

America became the target of terrorists. Arguments waged publicly back and forth blaming everything and everyone under the sun for the lead-up to 9/11 and the culmination of the final strikes.

Print, radio, and television media offered huge sums of money to experts in the field and to almost anyone else who appeared to have a handle on the cause of 9/11. Publishers courted journalists and others willing to author a book and I found a few books that, whether hastily written or not, whether their facts were true or not, helped fill in many of the blanks.

The selection of available books was eclectic, with some focusing on the terrorists' plans and build-up to the attacks, and others relating to who the al Qaeda zealots were and why they attacked the World Trade Center in New York City's lower Manhattan for the second time. Obviously they wanted to make as big a statement as possible and the globally-famous World Trade Center fit the bill. A third target included the Pentagon, and a fourth commercial airliner had been said to be heading for the White House but instead, thanks to the brave passengers who thwarted the hijackers, the pilot sent the plane nose-first into a Pennsylvania field.

I knew I had a lot of reading ahead.

Chapter 8

First and foremost on my list was the U.S. Government's official report, considered the most important paperback on the terrible event. "The 9/11 Commission Report" with the sub-title, "Final Report of the National Commission on Terrorist Attacks Upon the United States" published by W.W. Norton and priced at $10, had been eagerly awaited. The extraordinary 567-page Report released in 2004 was the work of ten Commission members and 128 staffers. Instead of a dry narrative expected from government bureaucrats the Report reads like a thriller. Painstakingly created by, it claims, an independent U.S. Government bi-partisan panel, the book examines the facts and circumstances surrounding the September 11 attacks. The Report headlines the first chapter with the cryptic statement, "We have some planes." The transmission was from American Airlines Flight 11 to ground control and sounded strange. What does the pilot mean? It soon became clear. The pilot was a hijacker. His remark was followed by the words,

"Just stay quiet, and you'll be okay. We are return-ing to the airport. Nobody move."

The conversations between the terrorist pilots and ground control were included in the book, whether from the pilots, the hijackers, the passen-gers, the crew, or personnel at the airports. A few of the airline controllers were taken completely by surprise; others were so puzzled by some of the re-marks sent their way that they couldn't grasp their significance. Only one or two caught on right away.

Particularly chilling were pages 30 and 31 that list the timeline of each plane from takeoff to the moment of crash. There were also quoted discus-sions between government agencies such as the FAA and military and law enforcement agencies.

The U.S. Government's publication provided detail after exact detail with dates, times, hundreds of names, and places where the terrorists lived and trained. A myriad of extraordinarily precise par-ticularities fill its pages. But were they true? Did the Commission twist some details to their own advantage? Although the Report is not without its detractors and critics despite what appears to the average reader to be meticulous research into the hijackers' movements and missions going back many years, several books were written question-ing its premise and presenting the authors' own ev-idence. One headline in a newspaper read: "Weak and Ill-Prepared," criticizing the conclusions of the key findings of the Commission.

Other media, too, excoriated the U.S. Government's unpreparedness for domestic and international anti-U.S. terrorism despite earlier bombings in Oklahoma, New York City, and against U.S. Government personnel and the military abroad. For my part I appreciated the Report's meticulous research that took me, as a reader, inside each of the first hour of the four flights. There are detailed descriptions of the hijackers passing through airport security before boarding, names and dates of where in America they trained as pilots, their backgrounds, and much more, all culminating in a report of book-length that is a massive compilation of relative information of the infamous day.

One of the first non-fiction books to be published after 9/11 was "Relentless Pursuit. The DSS and the Manhunt for the al Qaeda Terrorists" in 2003. It was written by author and journalist Samuel M. Katz. DSS stands for the Diplomatic Security Service tasked with protecting the security of the U.S. Department of State and its personnel serving abroad in embassies, consulates, and in other offices. The book's first chapter, titled "Signposts Along the Way," pointed to several events around the globe that Katz claimed led up to the hijackings in America and could or should have been recognized, validated and confirmed by the U.S. Government. The book noted that ever since the 1980s, terrorists have been living, visiting, and operating with relative ease in the United States.

"Signposts" ties in several anti-American bombings and attacks around the world with its climactic hijackings of four commercial airliners. Katz's personal interviews with some of the deadliest criminals and terrorists in the world make the reader's blood run cold. He also pointed to 1992 as the year al Qaeda went global. Sofia agreed with that conclusion when she met her hijacker husband in March, 1992 although at the time and for years later she was unaware, albeit suspicious, of his purpose or mission until September 11, 2001.

Another non-fiction book that pulled no punches was "The Big Wedding," by Sander Hicks which took the lid off the prevailing theories and accused the U.S. Government of having foreknowledge of 9/11. The author called the Commission Report a national disgrace and claimed the government allowed the attacks to happen as an excuse to engage in a war, and then fashioning a cover-up after the attacks on the Twin Towers and the other places where the hijackings occurred. Written in a breezy, familiar style its details were chilling with times, names, dates, places, copies of documents, and recorded quotes. The book was a superb and compelling record of facts and figures that Anthony Lappe, internationally-acclaimed journalist extraordinaire and producer, highly endorses in the book's Foreword.

The title Hicks chose for his book, "The Big Wedding," was the codename for the 9/11 attacks by some of the terrorists although he gives it his own interpretation by writing that "'The Big Wedding' is actually one between reality and the future, between a time of deceit and a time of truth, a time of permanent war, and the time for war to end permanently."

One disbelieving journalist pointed out that some of the hijackers would have been too old to be among the 9/11 terrorists, most of whom were said to be in their early twenties. However, some were identified as being in their late twenties and early-to-mid thirties, three of them the hijacker pilots. Karim was 31 years old in 2001.

Some years later, one of Hollywood's top screenwriters and authors, Thomas B. Sawyer, wrote a thriller, "No Place to Run," that also built on the idea that the president at the time, George W. Bush, and government agencies had been alerted ahead of time about the impending attacks and allowed them to happen. There were many, many theories propounded that led to both fiction and non-fiction books being published.

However, as a reporter I always wanted to know the small, personal, ordinary details, the human interest angle, behind such an event. I knew from the Report it required years of planning and plotting and the immense effort that the terrorists poured into its success. My work with Sofia presented an ideal opportunity for the behind-the-scenes background in addition to her desire to tell the story from her point of view. I hoped her book would be a form of catharsis, a letting-go of the miserable feelings of shame and guilt she knew she would never be able to totally release.

My reading list also included "The Cell," by John Miller and Michael Stone, with Chris Mitchell whom I took to be the actual writer of the book. Another account was "The Looming Tower," by Lawrence Wright who was able, astonishingly, to detail and trace the path of the 9/11 assault back to 1948. In an article he said that two of the hijackers had flown to the U.S. and settled in San Diego, a fact confirmed later by Sofia.

I searched online for other pertinent reports and found Steve Emerson's newsletter on his web site which provided a wealth of information. He was an American journalist, author and commentator who wrote and talked on terrorism, Islamic extremism, and about national security and its lack thereof. He was a regular expert on CNN, U.S. News and World Report, and many other media outlets. In 1993, the same year that Karim married Sofia, Emerson's documentary, "Terrorism Among Us: Jihad in America," was filmed. It aired on the Public Broadcasting Service in November, 1994, the same year that a divorced Sofia and her sister Anne visited the FBI offices in San Diego with, again, their warnings and which were summarily dismissed amid the Bureau's complacency.

Emerson's documentary specified that future terrorist attacks on the United States were in the offing, winning him the George Polk Award and other prizes and accolades. One wonders if anyone, anywhere in national law enforcement and similar services took any notice of the significant events leading up to September 11, 2001. As the writers pointed out in their books and articles after the attacks, albeit in hindsight, the writing had been on the wall for a long time for all to see.

Yet another book was by reporter Terry McDermott titled "Perfect Soldiers. The Hijackers. Who They Were and Why They Did it," which I read when it was published in 2005. The cover illustration of the hooded, heavily-lidded dead eyes of the Egyptian ringleader of the 9/11 attacks, Mohammed Atta, was provided courtesy of the Federal Bureau of Investigation according to the publisher. It is compelling, riveting and frightening. In Part III, Chapter 2, McDermott addresses the terrorists' activities while they were living in San Diego and their pretense of being college students. Sofia backed up these claims by telling the FBI and myself about the men taking flying lessons at a San Diego airport and bringing Middle Easterners across the Mexico-U.S. border after a night of clubbing in Tijuana.

While the content of these books were meticulous and disturbing reports of the events and what led up to them I realized that Sofia's story was comparatively different. Hers was a true recounting of how the terrorists spent their time each day at her home, of their enjoying a wild nightlife, of a personal look at their routine activities, shopping for clothes, their customs and habits when, as she noted grimly, they were not plotting to blow up America's landmarks and kill as many people as possible.

"Karim and his buddies claimed to practice Shariah law but in my presence they broke plenty of them," said Sofia. "I could understand why they smoked although it was banned. They were addicts and found it difficult to give up their cigarettes. Karim told me that some Arabs quit belonging to al Qaeda because they were too addicted."

Sofia's revelations were an account of her days and nights living with the cell members and their leader who gathered in her living room as if they were neighbors popping in for coffee or a beer. Her experiences were told to me from the viewpoint of an 18-year old wife of one of the terrorists who hijacked Flight 175, and later in retrospect when the horror and meaning of her past came back to haunt her.

With the hijackers' true identities laid out on the dining table in Erika's house, the sun streaming through the side window highlighting Cody's toy truck on the floor, the full impact of Sofia Wainwright's life with Karim ibn Riyad, or Aswad al Abadi as he was identified by the FBI, was sinking in.

"I knew I had to talk to the FBI," she told me later as I kept an eye on the cassette tape's progress. One time a tape had jammed while I was interviewing a previous client and I lost valuable material. "The Bureau told me that the terrorists arrived in America a year or two before the attack but I knew this was untrue. Some of those I met were in our country years before that, going back to the 1980s, just as District Attorney Terwilliger attested to later."

When I asked Sofia how her involvement with Karim began and when she first met him she stared off into the distance, blinking away the tears that slid down her cheeks. As she began to speak again I turned up the volume on my tape recorder and grabbed a pen and notepad. I needed to catch every word Sofia uttered about the consequences of her impulsive act as a high school senior.

"Sofia, let's start with the day you ran away from home."

Chapter 9

"Hurry up, sis, we'll be late for the school bus," said Jeff, poking his head around the door of the bedroom Sofia shared with her sister, Anne, before Anne left home. "Geez, what's in that huge duffel bag? You're not bringing that on the bus, are you?"

"Go on ahead," said Sofia. "I'm not going to school today."

"Oh, come on, sis, you've only got one more semester before graduation. Don't mess it up now."

"I'm sick of school."

"Sick of school? You almost made the Dean's List. You can get a college scholarship if you behave yourself. Everyone loves you in spite of the crazy stuff you pull."

Sofia laughed. "I know, Jeff. But I'm bored to tears here. I can't stand living in this place one second longer. Look, I'm going to tell you a secret, but you can't tell Mom."

Jeff came all the way into the room and closed the door behind him.

"A secret?"

"I'm going to run away this morning while Mom's out at that apartment house she manages. I've left her a note. I'm going to hitchhike to Portland and find Anne."

Jeff's mouth fell open. "Run away? Why would you want to do that? You're the most popular girl in school!"

Sofia shrugged. Just turned seventeen, she knew she was popular. She played the trumpet in the school band, sang in the choir, was always first on the dance floor, and was admired for a sweet nature. But she was also the wild one in the family. Restless, eager to explore the world, she was a leggy wildflower of a girl, strikingly beautiful. Her naturally blonde hair, blue eyes, flawless porcelain complexion, and tall slender body inherited from her Scandinavian mother gave Sofia the appearance of a willowy supermodel.

Two years earlier, in rebellion, she'd dyed her hair black to match the Goth clothes she wore, along with black lipstick and nail polish. When I interviewed Jeff he described how she changed her hair color every other month, it seemed, from blonde to black, then red, and back to blonde.

He said Sofia was a talented artist and won every art class award at school. He told me that she used to draw hearts in her text books and doodled all over her schoolbooks. She even etched her name onto the teacher's oak desk.

47

"She was the creative one of the family, and was always laughing. She seemed to light up everything around her," he said.

When she was a sophomore Sofia had also taken to using methamphetamine. Readily available in the small town where drug addicts ranged from teens to senior citizens and residents manufactured the drug in home labs, meth was as common as Marlboros. A school friend introduced Sofia to the narcotic and they both enjoyed the excitement and potential danger that went along with smoking it.

Stealing a few bucks from Erika's purse now and then to fund a drug purchase Sofia nevertheless decided to quit using meth after several weeks. She quit being a Goth, too, throwing out her black lipstick and other macabre looks, and the dark music of bands such as Play Dead, Bauhaus, Specimen, and the U.K.'s Decay. She dropped her black eye make-up into the garbage, and bought hair products to revert to her blonde hair.

She was the last of six children abandoned by their father when she was eight-years old. After he left the large family needed a parent at home to care for them all, forcing Erika to leave her executive job with the nation's premier sewing machine company and take on part-time jobs, mostly working night shifts.

Well-known locally as a skilled dress designer and professional tailor Erika nevertheless brought in barely enough money to support the children.

She spent long hours at home sewing garments for local customers, many of whom were themselves living on limited incomes. Finally, Erika found a permanent job as the night manager of an apartment building, and her older sons worked at after-school odd jobs to help make ends meet.

By the beginning of the 1990s three of the children were grown and leaving home. The oldest daughter, Heather, had already left to get married and was living in South Carolina. Ben and Alan had also married and were working in other states while still in their early twenties. Anne, at nineteen, was in Portland working at a McDonald's restaurant. Only Jeff and Sofia were still at home and attending school.

"So, you are really running away? Wow!" said Jeff. "Mom's gonna be real mad."

"I don't care. I'm going," said Sofia. "I have dreams. I want to find out what's out there and have adventures. I want to live instead of being stuck in the sticks in this backward burg."

She finished packing the navy nylon duffel bag, closed its zipper, and picked it up

"Mom's going to hit the roof," said Jeff, grinning at the prospect.

"She'll get over it. I've left her a note. You know how guilty I feel about embarrassing her all the time by smoking and other stuff. Maybe Mom would be better off without me. I just can't conform like everyone else."

Jeff stared at her and shook his head. "You're so stubborn. Okay, I know for sure I can't change your mind. So, how about I walk you to the I-5 and make sure you get a safe ride?"

"You'll miss the school bus."

"Don't worry about it."

Chapter 10

I pressed the tab to stop the tape recorder and suggested to Sofia that we take a break. We'd returned to her mother's home, worked for four hours, had a quick late lunch, and resumed our work. At 5 p.m. we went out for an early dinner. Erika recommended the Panda Express, saying that it served excellent, reasonably-priced food.

As we ate I asked Sofia if she'd had any qualms about hitchhiking alone. The Green River murders in the Seattle, Washington State area were still unsolved in the 1990s. She laughed and reminded me she'd been too naive and innocent at the time to believe any harm could befall her. She had lived a relatively sheltered life in a family that practiced a Christian religion as Jehovah's Witnesses. Unfamiliar with it I asked Sofia to give me a brief explanation. It had strict rules, all of which she broke, she said. By the time she was a 16-year old her behavior was censured.

"It's a beautiful religion that I practice now with fervor but back then I didn't care. I shamed my mother with my bad actions and activities," she said. "By the time I left home I would probably have been ex-communicated by them anyway."

"Tell me more."

"We honor Jehovah, the God of the bible and the creator of all things. We imitate Christ and each of us spends time helping others learn about the bible and God's Kingdom. The Witnesses are peacefully anti-government. We don't salute the flag nor sing the National Anthem. I was taught that we did not vote or join the military. In fact, we were to remain neutral in every aspect of American life. No celebrating holidays except Passover."

"Why the word 'Witnesses?'"

"Because," she said, "each of us is a witness to Almighty God, whose name is Jehovah. We believe that God, as Christ, was raised from the dead as an immortal spirit person."

"Just how strict is it?"

Sofia explained that their mother, Erika, would circle in the newspaper's TV Guide schedule which shows the children were allowed to watch. Among them were "The Dukes of Hazzard," "Little House on the Prairie," and "Grizzly Adams."

There were other rules, some of which she was usually the first sibling to break but, she assured me, nothing dreadful, just kid's stuff like smoking, refusing to clean the bedroom she shared with Anne, and minor infractions. Crime was almost unknown in Dundee. She, along with most of the residents, could not imagine anything as horrific as kidnappings and killings happening in their quiet, rural town.

"There are drugs, sure, and petty theft but nothing more serious than a drunken hit-and-run now and then, and some mild domestic violence. Occasionally there are a couple of break-ins for money. The only murders we heard about happened a couple of years ago, a home invasion robbery that went wrong and the couple in the house were shot."

We returned to Erika's home and Sofia continued her story.

The elderly driver of the battered Ford pickup pulled over to the curb and turned to Sofia on the passenger seat.

"This is the center of Portland, right here, miss. You sure you're going to be all right?"

"Oh, yes, and thank you so much. You've been very kind," she said, getting out of the vehicle and buttoning her jacket against the cool wind. "I'll soon find my sister. Everything'll be okay."

She closed the vehicle's door and went to the back of the truck to retrieve her duffel bag. She gave the driver a cheery wave as he drove off. Nice guy, she thought. Old, though. Must be at least forty or so, nothing like the dream man I intend to marry. He'll drive a flashy Dodge truck or a nice Chevy four-door like our sales manager neighbor back in Dundee.

Sofia looked around at the bustling sidewalks, the traffic crowding the streets, the shops, the two hotels she'd just passed, and breathed deeply. Man, was she going to enjoy living here. This was heaven. Now, where's the nearest McDonald's? All she knew of her sister's place of work was the name of the fast food restaurant.

It had been over a year since Anne left home, striking out on her own. Like Sofia, her older sister wanted to shake the dust of Dundee off her shoes. After graduating from high school she'd headed for the big city. Once in Portland she'd let her family know she was settled and after that she only called home on her mother's birthday.

Sofia entered a diner and asked if they had a pay phone and a Yellow Pages directory. Directed to a side wall where the heavy phone book was hanging from a string attached to the phone, her heart sank when she flipped hastily through the pages and saw several listings for McDonald's.

"Oh, no. I'm in trouble. There must 20 of them here," she mumbled.

Sofia only had three quarters in her purse. Each call cost 25 cents. Which three restaurants should she choose? She tried to remember anything Anne might have told her about her job but nothing came to mind. She picked three at random, two of them on the same street but many blocks apart. Sofia wasn't even sure her sister was still working at the same job or if it might be her day off. If that was the case, where would she sleep?

Anne did not work at any of the three McDonald's she called. Checking the phone book again she selected three more that she could walk to, and trudged down the street looking for the first place on her list, asking passers-by for directions and cross streets. After she walked five more blocks she saw a McDonald's sign. With a sigh of relief, she went inside, dropped the duffel bag onto a wooden seat in the nearest empty booth and went up to the counter, smiling at the woman behind one of the cash registers.

"Does Anne Wainwright work here?" she asked.

The woman frowned. "Anne Wainwright? Not as far as I know. She's not on my shift, that's for sure. Wait a minute, I'll ask the manager if he knows the name."

Sofia was grateful for the courtesy. See, she told herself, it's not scary here in the big city. I'm psyched! She waited anxiously for the woman to return from the back of the restaurant.

"No, sorry. We don't know anyone with that name who works here. Maybe she's at our East Portland location, or one of the others."

"Oh, dear. Could you call around to them and ask?"

"Sorry, I can't do that, but there's a pay phone around the corner, to your left."

"Oh, I don't have any more money."

As Sofia's eyes teared up the cashier took some coins from a nearby tip jar. "Here, this should help."

Sofia accepted four quarters, thanking the woman for her kindness and rushing to the phone. She dialed one of the numbers on the list.

"Is Anne Wainwright there, please? She is?" Sofia almost dropped the receiver in her excitement. "Oh, that's wonderful. Tell her that her sister will be right over. No, change that. Don't say anything. I want to surprise her. Are you downtown? Oh, near the Shelley and Greene department store. Great. Can you give me directions from the McDonald's on West Burnside to your restaurant, please?"

She repeated the directions she was told, hung up the phone, ran over to the cashier who'd helped her, gave her back the remaining quarters, and thanked her again. Sofia grabbed her bag and left. I'm on my way, she thought. Life, here I come!

Chapter 11

Sofia laughed as she told me she practically ran the several blocks to her destination, looking ahead for the yellow arch with the name of the restaurant in bright red. The duffel bag was weighing her down, she said, but she felt elated.

"I'm in the big city," she murmured, craning her neck to see the tops of Portland's high-rise buildings. "I love it."

She gave a little skip, walked a few paces, ran, slowed down, and skipped again, thrilled to be at the start of her adventure. The family's only excursion out of Dundee had been to Disneyland when she was ten years old. Erika had saved up for three years to take all of her children to the theme park and they'd talked about the trip for almost as long afterwards.

Finding McDonald's, Sofia opened the door and stood inside for a moment, looking around. There appeared to be several students sitting at the tables and booths with books scattered around, some studying, others laughing and talking. A few were darker-skinned and Sofia wondered which country they came from. Mexico, she decided.

She spotted Anne behind the counter giving a customer change from the till. Her sister still wore her strawberry blonde hair in a long ponytail, her blue eyes matching Sofia's own. Despite the bulky uniform and surrounded by burgers and fries, Anne's figure was still trim. After her customer picked up his order and went to a table, Sofia approached.

"Anne. Hey, look who's come to Portland!" Her broad grin lit up her face as she waited anxiously for approval from her older sister.

"Sofia, oh, my goodness. What are you doing here? Is Mom with you? And Jeff?"

"Nope. I've run away. I left a note for Mom. Can I stay with you?"

"You've really run away? Oh, my God. Well, it doesn't surprise me, knowing you. But first we'd better call home and let them know you're safe. Mom will be so worried, even though you said you left a note. We don't want her calling the cops."

Sofia made the call on the pay phone and assured her frantic mother she was fine and would be staying with Anne. Back at the counter her sister picked up a tray holding a soda, a wrapped burger and fries, and handed it to Sofia.

"Here," Anne said. "You can sit with my boyfriend, Stefan, in that first booth, and his friend," she said, pointing. "Stefan's the good-looking one with the red scarf. I think the other guy's name is Karim. He's from the Middle East somewhere."

Sofia took the tray and walked over to the booth Anne indicated.

"Hi, Stefan. I'm Sofia, Anne's sister. She said I should sit with you. Is that okay?" She smiled at the other young man sitting in the booth who nodded but otherwise barely acknowledged her presence and quickly looked away.

Stefan, too, nodded and smiled but said nothing, continuing to make notes from a text book open on the table. Students, figured Sofia, sitting down. Must be a college nearby. She liked the curly black hair that spilled past Stefan's shoulders, the hazel eyes, and tentative grin. His sweat shirt and jeans, though, were in marked contrast to his companion's appearance whose swarthy complexion, polished nails, and the gold pen he was using told her this was no poor local American student. His facial features were much darker than Stefan's and she wondered where he was from in the Middle East. She knew her geography and often dreamed of traveling to the lands of the exotic names she read in the school's international atlas. After a few minutes the man got up and left without saying another word.

Sofia was almost finished with her meal before her sister came over and sat next to her in the booth.

"It's my break time," Anne explained. She turned to her boyfriend. "Stefan, Sofia will be staying with me for a while." She gave her sister a hug. "It'll be a tight fit, it's just a studio apartment and I already have a roommate, Lorna, but she's away a lot. We'll manage. I'm so glad to see you. I was feeling kind of lonely with no family around but now here you are."

"When do you get off?"

"In two hours so just sit tight till I'm done."

Stefan soon gathered up his books and note-pads, stood up, waved to them both, and left.

"What's the story with your boyfriend? I guess he's a student," said Sofia as soon as Stefan was out of earshot.

"He's studying English at Portland State University."

"Where's he from?"

"Romania."

"Wow!"

Anne laughed. "There are lots of foreign students in Portland, especially wealthy ones from the Middle East. They come in here all the time. They love fast food. Most of them go to Lewis and Clark College or Portland State University."

"Is Stefan wealthy?"

"No," said Anne. "He's here on a scholarship and whatever money his parents in Romania can scrape together for him. But we have fun without much money."

"Do you think I could get a job here?"

"Let's get you settled first then we'll figure out what you want to do. With your looks you could work in an upscale department store, and with your brains I bet you could easily move up to a managerial position."

"Are there buses from your place to get downtown?"

"Of course. Here, take this. You can pay me back from your first week's salary." Anne handed Sofia a $20 bill. "And take these quarters, you'll be needing them for the bus when you get a job."

"Can I stay with you until I get work and find my own place?"

"Sure, but it's only a studio apartment, as I said. I have a full-sized bed that you and I will have to share. Lorna, sleeps on the pull-out sofa. It's cramped but we manage. I wish you'd waited till after graduation and got your diploma but I know how impulsive you are."

"Heck, Anne, I'd just had it, that's all. Mom was always so mad at me. The teachers were, too. Yeah, all my fault, I know, but I don't care about school when there's so many exciting things to explore. I'll never go back to Dundee."

Chapter 12

Although March was Portland's rainiest month Sofia spent the next few days exploring, wandering around the city on her own, and window-shopping. At Pioneer Plaza one store displayed teen mannequins dressed in neon-colored dresses that were popular at the time. If I get a job in this store, she thought, I'll be able to buy those clothes at a discount, according to Anne.

Her sister told her she'd help her create a resume when she had her day off. In the meantime Sofia familiarized herself with the city, walking everywhere or riding the buses. She found a spot on the bank of the Willamette River to watch the water traffic and at four o'clock each afternoon she made her way to McDonald's to accompany Anne home after work.

Whenever Stefan was at the restaurant Sofia sat with him. On the fifth day while she waited for Anne to finish her shift he asked her in halting English if she'd like to go on a date with his best friend, Karim.

"He is student like me, the one you see when you first came."

"Oh, the guy in the beautiful clothes who didn't want to speak to me?"

"Yes. From Middle East. He come here sometimes but likes pizza place better."

"I'll ask Anne and see what she thinks," said Sofia. "She still calls me her baby sister, you know."

"We go Caliber nightclub. Dancing music. Much fun."

Sofia eyes sparkled. Finally, she'd get a taste of big city life. She rushed over to Anne behind the counter.

"Hey, Stefan has asked me to meet his friend, Karim, on a blind date, the one that was here before. He's from the Middle East. Imagine that! We'll all go dancing. Please say yes, Anne."

"Karim? I've met him. He's not my favorite kind of guy."

"How old is he?" said Sofia.

"He's a student so I'd say, twenty-one or twenty-two. He's from a wealthy family in Saudi Arabia, I think. He's not a deadbeat, that's for sure. He acts pretty uppity, though, and he's really stuck on himself."

"Uppity? I'll soon bring him down to size. You know how outspoken I am. Come on, Anne, we're double-dating and that means you'll be able to keep an eye on me. Anyway, I want to go to that club."

"Okay, okay but I sure will be keeping an eye on you on the dance floor. The Arab students can get pretty grabby."

Back at the studio apartment Sofia rummaged through her duffel bag. She'd brought her one and only Sunday dress, a turquoise velvet that her mother designed when the family attended a cousin's wedding. Sofia had also packed a black miniskirt she'd hemmed herself after cutting off six inches from the knee-length skirt Erika had made. She pulled from the bag two black cotton blouses; an extra pair of jeans, and her well-worn black pumps.

"Shall I wear my dress or this black skirt and blouse?" Sofia asked Anne.

"Certainly not that Goth stuff, and the dress is far too formal, more for a fancy restaurant than a club. Take a look in my closet, we're the same size."

"Oh, can I? You are definitely, absolutely, fantastically wonderful." Sofia jumped up and down a couple of times and opened the closet. "I'm so excited! Oh, I love this red skirt." She took out a short, flared red miniskirt and held it against her.

"There's a top to match it next to the green blouse. Try them on. And stop jumping, the old couple downstairs will be after us."

"Sorry. I keep forgetting I'm almost grown up. Oh, this outfit looks terrific." She pirouetted in front of Anne's fill-length mirror propped again the wall. "Thanks. Can I borrow those red shoes? And I'm going to wear my hair up," she said, sweeping her long braids into a circle around her head.

"Sure, take the shoes. But leave your hair loose and down," said Anne. "These guys love blondes with long waves like yours."

"But I look older when I wear my hair up."

"Suit yourself. I'm just telling you what I know."

"Okay. What kind of club are we going to?" asked Sofia. "Stefan said there was dancing."

"One of the newest, Caliber. It's real trendy. You won't be allowed to drink, of course, because of the liquor laws and you are under age but you can have a soda."

"No problem. I'll be dancing all the time."

Chapter 13

As soon as they entered the club through the dimly-lit entryway the deejay music hit their ears like an explosion. Red and green fluorescent lights flashed off and on, couples gyrated on the packed dance floor, and Nirvana's hit single, "Smells Like Teen Spirit," caused Sofia to start jiving as she and Anne passed by the curved bar, every stool taken and patrons three deep.

"This is heaven," Sofia shouted into her sister's ear. "Hope they'll play some Pearl Jam and R.E.M. rock, too. So, where are the guys?"

"Upstairs, in the lounge."

Anne indicated a flight of wide marble steps that led to a mezzanine. She took Sofia's hand, smiling at the look of wonderment on her sister's face as her eyes darted everywhere, taking it all in. Yep, nothing like this in Dundee.

At the top of the stairs Anne turned left and approached a grouping of red leather loveseats encircling a drum-shaped black lacquer coffee table where Stefan and Karim were sitting and talking.

The table held tall drink glasses, half-empty, and four beer bottles bearing the labels of one of Portland's many custom breweries.

Stefan stood up but Karim remained seated, staring at Sofia who was surprised he didn't get to his feet. Foreigners, she thought, they sure do have different customs to us.

"Karim, this is my sister Sofia, you met her at McDonald's remember?"

The man nodded. "Yes."

Sofia disliked him on sight. She stretched out her hand to shake his, noting in one quick but all-encompassing glance the well-tailored clothes, the salmon-pink turtleneck under an unbuttoned white shantung silk jacket. She glimpsed black dress pants pleated at the waist and accessorized by a braided leather belt. He wore a heavy gold watch on his wrist. Sofia saw that his grooming was impeccable including the manicured nails. He nodded and with an arm gesture, invited her to sit next to him. Anne and Stefan were already immersed in a private conversation.

Sofia waited for Karim to begin talking but he seemed tongue-tied. He kept staring at her in what she perceived was an aloof manner. She felt as if his dark eyes were penetrating her soul, she told Anne later. Yet, despite a long, droopy nose she acknowledged to herself that he was handsome in an exotic, foreign way.

While Stefan was robust and well-built Karim appeared thin in contrast, his beautifully-tailored clothes failing to hide narrow shoulders and a slight frame. His neck was scrawny and there seemed to be little substance to him. He appeared, in fact, to be almost delicate. Yet Sofia felt a certain power, a silent confidence in him that intrigued her. Maybe, she thought, all rich foreigners have this air about them. Sofia was expecting a fun-loving flirtatious companion. Instead, he was aloof, holding his head up stiffly. What does he have that justifies him having his nose in the air, she thought. On the other hand maybe he is from a royal family somewhere.

After ordering canapes and drinking more beer Stefan and Anne took to the dance floor. Sofia turned to Karim expectantly.

"Don't you dance?" she said.

"Not."

"Not? Do you mean, no?" Sofia decided to have a little fun with him. "You've barely said a word since I got here. What are you studying? Where do you come from? Have you been here long? Where are you living?"

She fired the questions off at double speed, enjoying his discomfort. How could Stefan have fixed her up with this moron?

"Come on." Sofia stood up, pulling on Karim's hand. "We need to dance."

Reluctantly, he got up from the sofa and followed her slowly onto the dance floor. She noticed that he was almost an inch shorter than her 5 ft. 8 in. height, which made him appear all the more frail. She was used to being around well-built lumbermen in Dundee like her father and the neighbors.

Knowing all the latest moves from watching Anne's television Sofia was soon twisting, bobbing, and swaying in rhythm to the music as the neon lights flashed different colors. Karim tried to copy her. He jerked his arms around and bent his knees so awkwardly that Sofia had to stifle a laugh but by now she didn't care. She was having the most fun she'd ever had.

Chapter 14

When they arrived home after saying goodbye to Stefan and Karim, Anne asked her sister what she thought of her date.

"I guess he's an Arab, right?" Sofia shrugged, her mouth turned down at the corners in a grimace. "He must have a lot of money to be wearing those clothes."

"What do you know about men's clothes aside from the jeans and denim shirts everyone wears in Dundee? You've never gone farther than twenty miles outside of town except for our trip to Disneyland when we were kids."

"I know, Anne, but I read all those fashion magazines that Mom gets in the mail and sometimes copies their illustrations. And I read the pricey fashion magazines in the library that anyone can read for free."

"But tell me honestly, what do you think of Karim?" said Anne

"Not much. Sorry, but he was arrogant. He didn't even loosen up on the dance floor. He has no sense of rhythm and tried to twist his skinny ole body as if he was made of quicksilver. Dumb. He looked ridiculous. I think he said all of two words the whole evening. What's he about?"

Anne shrugged. "It's not surprising when you consider he speaks hardly any English. I guess I forgot to tell you that he's shy about talking. He's here to learn the language, you know. I still don't like him, either, but give him a chance if you want."

"No way. I expected to be set up with a blind date who was happy and knows how to enjoy himself, not someone who didn't even try to flirt with me. He's all sharp angles, bony, and there's something unsettling about him. When he did talk he bragged about many Arabs were now in America and how easy it is to get student visas. So what? America's full of foreigners and immigrants."

Sofia added she was turned off by his imperious attitude but his elegant worldliness and the mysterious undercurrents she detected in his personality intrigued her.

"Anne, I have to admit that his clothes are gorgeous. That silk sweater was stunning. Was it Italian? Wish Mom could see it, you know how she appreciates European designer clothes."

Lorna, Anne's roommate, looked up at Sofia and Anne from the book she was reading. A short, young woman in her twenties with waist-length auburn hair and green eyes, she was sprawled on the daybed pushed up against the wall in one corner of the studio apartment.

"You had a date with Karim?" she said. "Geez, stay away from him. He's disgusting. He took me to a strip joint and spent all night throwing hundred-dollar bills over a dancer's bosom and stuffing money into another dancer's panties. It was gross."

Anne laughed. "Lorna, was that your first time at a strip club? The dancers always come around afterwards and you're supposed to put money into their panties or into those wide belts or whatever they're wearing. Everyone knows that."

"Not me, and yes, it was my first time. Those moves the girls made on the dance floor were much too vulgar. They were even feeling themselves up. It was so embarrassing."

Sofia smiled. "Really? I'd have gotten up and danced myself. I'd give those girls a run for their money. Oh, don't look so shocked, Anne," she said, seeing her sister's expression. "Life's about trying something new, having a good time."

"I see you've brought your wild ways with you," said Anne. "They're going to get you into trouble if you don't watch out."

Chapter 15

The next day, as the sisters discussed Sofia's immediate problem of finding a job now that the resume had been composed and several copies made, Stefan called.

"Good morning, dearest Anne," he said. "Good fun last night. Now, Karim he want Sofia to go on date. Only two. Him and her. What do you think?"

Anne frowned. "A date with Karim? She's only 17, Stefan. Alone?" She looked at her sister, eyebrows raised in question.

Sofia shook her head vigorously side to side. No way, she mouthed. Anne talked into the phone.

"She isn't keen on him, Stefan. I'd say no."

"But he wants it," said Stefan.

"Too bad. Oh, heavens. Look at the time. I have to go. See you later."

Anne hung up the phone and said goodbye to Sofia and Lorna. Before she went out the door she suggested that Sofia spend the day applying for work in person at the department stores downtown near the McDonald's where she worked. She pointed out that with her sister's good looks she'd make a great saleslady and that she should choose a conservative outfit to wear from Anne's closet.

"Come by at lunch time and give me a report on your progress."

"Yes, ma'am," smiled Sofia, giving her sister a salute. "Orders received and understood."

Anne smiled back and said, "You're going to have to face reality, Sofia. You need a job if you stay here."

"I know, I know. It's just that......"

"Oops, I'm off. See you."

Sofia, demure in Anne's navy suit and pale blue blouse that matched her eyes, walked into McDonald's. She immediately saw Anne at the counter and approached her, staying quiet until the customer Anne was giving change to stood aside to wait for his order.

"Hey, sis, I got asked back to meet the sales manager at their evening gown department at Sainsbury's on Friday."

"That's great, Sofia. You look terrific in my suit but we'll have to figure out what you can wear for the second interview. I don't have much in the way of appropriate dresses. Well, we have a couple of days to figure it out. Maybe Lorna has something you can borrow, she's shorter but about your size and as she works in a doctor's clinic she has some nice clothes. Her skirts will be above the knee for you but you have great legs. Now, go and sit with Stefan in the last booth over there."

Sofia turned and saw Anne's boyfriend was sitting with Karim in the booth Anne indicated. Oh, no. She was about to head for the exit to leave when Stefan called out loudly to her and got up. He took her arm and steered her back to the booth. She sat down. Damn, I hope that Arab doesn't ask me out, she thought, I'll make sure I speak slowly so that he understands exactly that I am turning him down.

The man in question was wearing a light tan silk suit with wide lapels and closed by a single button. His shirt was black with a high collar starkly set off by a wide, white triangular Windsor-knotted tie. Who does he think he is, a Mafia gangster, thought Sofia, amused by the outfit that was totally out of place in the fast food restaurant filled with jeans-clad students. He was about to take a bite of a double cheeseburger when Stefan brought her to the table. Karim instantly put the food down, wiped his fingers on a napkin, and stood up. A cheek-to-cheek smile showed perfect teeth.

"Good day," he said, both arms outstretched. "Sit, please."

Sofia was taken aback by his enthusiasm. Not the surly man of last night. She shook his hand and sat beside Stefan. Across the table she could smell Karim's fragrant after-shave lotion and noted, as she had last night, the wavy hair combed to cover a receding hairline. The Arab's dark eyes again looked intently into her own and this time she felt a jolt of excitement pass through her.

"Tell me about your country," Sofia said to cover her feelings, knowing she was blushing.

"When speak better English, yes?"

"Hey, Sofia, why you don't help him with English, be teacher?" said Stefan, putting his arm around her. "He needs you. He arrive here three months ago only."

"But aren't you both studying our language in college?"

"Yes, but my English now improving much because I love Anne. She tell me good words." He laughed heartily. "You teach Karim. Tell him good words. Very intelligent guy."

"Then he will learn quickly," she said. "In class."

As she spoke Karim's still-intense scrutiny of her increased, his eyes unblinking. She decided he wasn't so bad after all, certainly far more a man of the world than the immature high school boys she knew and dated back in Dundee. Karim was the first real foreigner she'd ever met and he was from the mysterious Middle East. How cool was that?

"So, you take dinner with Karim tomorrow night?" said Stefan.

Had these guys set this all up beforehand? If they had, so what, she thought.

"I'll talk to Anne. She may have plans for us," said Sofia.

She got up and, practically bouncing on her toes, went to the counter where her sister was still working. "Guess what? Karim really wants to take me out to dinner tomorrow, like Stefan told you on the phone this morning, and I've decided I want to go after all."

"Alone?"

"Of course alone." Sofia frowned at Anne.

"I don't think it's a good idea. He's much more sophisticated than you. You're too young. Besides, he goes to those nude clubs. No. Definitely not."

"Well, I'm going and that's that."

Sofia tossed her blonde hair, turned away and went back to the table.

"Okay," she said to Karim. "You can pick me up tonight at Anne's."

Chapter 16

My recorder clicked, signaling the end of the cassette tape. I took it out, labeled it and inserted a fresh one.

"Sounds like you have a stubborn streak," I remarked to Sofia. "It was your first time in the big city. Didn't you think you should take it slowly?"

She laughed, a full-throated sound.

"Anne and I had quite an argument about Karim when we got home, which made me dig my heels in all the more. I was pretty contrary back then and Lorna's opinion and disapproval only made me more determined to do what I wanted. Besides, it was such an adventure to go out with a glamorous man like that. I was tingling with anticipation all day. I couldn't wait for the following night to get all dolled up."

Dressed in a collarless dark blue Armani suit with its distinctive slit pockets, Karim arrived at Anne's apartment at the agreed-upon time of eight o-clock that evening. He knocked on the door and waited until Sofia came out, then ushered her down the stairs and onto the tan leather passenger seat of his black 1992 Buick Roadmaster, the brand's latest sedan. Sofia tucked the skirt of her velvet dress around her as she sat down, conscious of its conservative style but proud of her mother's tailoring that could have displayed perfectly in any French couturier's salon.

"Where are we going?" said Sofia.

"My very popular restaurant. It is Jaipur House."

"You mean your 'favorite' restaurant, not 'popular.'"

She looked at him and laughed, expecting him to join in but his expression barely changed. Had she offended him by pointing out his mistake? Well, if she had, too bad. He was in America to learn English and that's what she was trying to do, help him with the language. Besides, where was his sense of humor?

Maybe this evening won't be so much fun after all, she thought. She had to admit she felt nervous about this first date with an older man. At seventeen she found the idea of going out with anyone over twenty, as Stefan estimated Karim's age at 21, was the height of delicious and dangerous folly. But Karim was like no one she'd ever met. To her, he was a sophisticated man whose exotic, foreign background intrigued her. She wanted to know more about him and his Arab friends. Maybe she could teach him to laugh.

At the restaurant she looked around eagerly at the diners. Flattered and excited that he'd brought her to one of Portland's most famous and elegant eateries downtown, she'd been surprised when the maitre d' hurried forward to greet Karim by name and led the couple to a large circular booth. The place was packed. Karim told her that he ate there almost every night and his table was always kept open for him and his friends.

Most of the patrons were Middles Eastern, some of the women in brightly-colored saris or Western cocktail dresses and the men in business suits of subtly iridescent fabrics. There were no women in Arab wear. In fact, most of the men were accompanied by blondes. Sofia studied the exotic paintings on the restaurant walls depicting some of India's mythical gods, goddesses, and ancient ruins.

A small dance floor was at the back of the room with an area on the perimeter occupied by two drummers and a percussionist. A belly dancer, her long black hair woven intricately into braids and small brass cymbals on the fingers of each hand, entered the dance floor. She wore a jeweled bra and a gold-studded belt around her hips holding up full-length harem pants of scarlet chiffon. When the music started she moved sinuously through her routine. Bending and rolling her body, her hips circling and undulating, Sofia saw that she mesmerized every male in the room.

Soon, another belly dancer joined her and they shimmied in faster and faster movements as the musicians increased the tempo. They finally stopped after a crescendo of drums, bowed to the diners, and went around the tables inviting patrons to stuff dollar bills into their clothing. Karim was polite and handed each dancer three hundred-dollar bills which they took and added to the money in their belts. There was none of the bravado and wild behavior that Lorna said he displayed on her date with him.

"To me, having lived such a different rural life, my evening at Jaipur House was all wonderfully new and exciting. I have to admit I was in awe," she told me.

Their waiter handed them both a menu but Karim shook his head, taking the menu from Sofia.

"I order."

Relieved, knowing she had no idea what the dishes were and pleasantly surprised that he was taking charge, she nodded.

"Yes, please. This is all new to me."

"Sofia," he replied, smiling. "You are …what, refreshing, is that good word? And honest. I like."

She smiled in return and cocked her head to one side, considering him. "You know, Karim, you're pretty okay yourself. You're different from the other night."

"When we know better, I am wonderful."

As she laughed he reached across the table and took her hand, squeezing it gently and stroking her fingers.

"No manicure? Tomorrow I take."

When Sofia related the details of that evening to me she gazed off into the distance. I checked the tape recorder to make sure it was still running.

"Victoria, he was like a movie star with his elegant clothes and his air of total self-confidence. He obviously felt completely at home in the big-bucks restaurant filled with rich-looking people. I felt like a princess, or more likely Cinderella as I was wearing my one and only dress. For all I knew, maybe he was a prince, or at least minor royalty! I sure had stars in my stupid eyes."

After they left Jaipur House, Karim suggested driving along the Willamette River. Lights sparkled off the water from both riverbanks and a crescent moon in a clear night sky illuminated the park that ran the length of downtown. A dozen bridges, built close together, crossed the Willamette. Karim took the Burnside Bridge, pointing out one of its neighbors, the double-decked Steel Bridge that carried trains and streetcars. He told Sofia that it linked the Rose Quarter and Lloyd District to the east and Portland's Old Town Chinatown area to the west.

"Those steel towers sure are huge," Sofia said. "Guess that's how the bridge got its name. But you only arrived here three months ago, Karim.

How come you know so much about these bridges?"

He took his left hand from the steering wheel and waved his arm around. "I study. I like American building. Very different to my country."

He didn't comment further as she chatted on, marveling at the bridge's height. He appeared to sink into deep thought and Sofia left him to it, gazing out of the window at Portland's skyline and twinkling lights.

Karim glanced at her now and then as he was driving. Apparently coming to a decision he headed for Anne's apartment and pulled up to the curb. He exited the car, went around to the passenger door, and helped Sofia out.

"Tomorrow night, 9 o'clock. We go to Candy Club."

After watching the Buick drive away Sofia raced up the stairs to fill Anne in on her dinner with Karim and his plans for the next date.

"The Candy Club?" said Anne. "That's a pretty notorious strip joint. I don't think you should go. You'll be out all night and you need to be looking good for that job interview."

"Of course I am going!"

Sofia flounced into the bathroom, removed her make-up, changed into a T-shirt, and slid into bed with her face turned away from Anne.

How different from home, she thought. How exciting my life has suddenly become. Anne is foolish to worry.

Chapter 17

The Candy Club's dance floor was shoulder-to-shoulder when Karim and Sofia emerged from the narrow, semi-dark lobby into the club itself. They were immediately greeted by a tall, barrel-chested man whose bald head shone in the half-light.

"Wonderful to see you here again, sir" he said to Karim, holding out his hand. "Your friends are at your usual table."

Sofia's heart sank. She wanted to spend time alone with her date and get to know him better. On the stage high above and at the back of the dance floor were four strippers winding their bodies erotically around silver poles that reached to the ceiling. Sofia was mesmerized by their moves as Karim led her to a table that was situated front and center.

Three Arabs were already seated and greeted Karim with nods. Karim didn't introduce Sofia but pulled out a chair for her and sat beside her. He snapped his fingers at a waiter and ordered beer for them both. Sofia expected him to hold her hand or put his arm around her as he had last night but he did neither. His religion or customs, she reflected, might prohibit public gestures of affection or he's embarrassed in front of his friends. Anne had already filled her in about some Middle Eastern behavior she'd picked up at McDonald's, whilst also telling her that Arabs often broke the club rules by hassling the dancers.

Karim didn't suggest they dance and two hours later, after watching the strippers, Sofia said she wanted to go home. She was tired. She hadn't enjoyed herself as much as she hoped and with Karim's full attention on the stage and speaking with his Arab friends in his own language, which sounded harsh to her, she felt neglected.

Sofia was pleased when, giving her no argument, Karim immediately called for the bill and the couple left the club. He drove her home but this time he didn't get out of the car to open her door. Maybe he's going to give me the heave-ho, she thought. Maybe it's over. But I can't pretend I was enjoying myself tonight. She looked at his profile as he stared out of the windshield.

"What is it?" she said.

Karim turned towards her and took her hand.

"Come with me."

"Where?" she said.

"I show."

He drove towards the river and parked outside an apartment building on Front Street at McCormick

Pier on the Willamette River. Nearby was the McCall Waterfront Park, the Saturday market, and the Pearl District. Its former industrial warehouses had been turned into art galleries and upscale lofts in the 1980s and its prime location was a mere mile to downtown Portland.

Karim led her to an elevator and what she assumed was the front door to his apartment. They went inside. Sofia was instantly impressed with the lavish furnishings, the colorful red and black Persian rugs, and the sumptuous sectional sofa covered in intricately-designed fabric slipcovers she figured were Middle Eastern. A large ornamental brass coffee table held several espresso coffee cups, the dregs still in the bottom. Against the far wall, along half of its entire length, was an aquarium. She walked towards it. As she got closer Sofia saw it was empty of water. All the tank contained was a pile of several large misshapen rocks on the bottom.

"No fish?" she said.

Karim smiled. "Look close. Behind big rock in middle."

She walked behind the tank and instantly recoiled. A 5 ft. long snake was curled up into a ball against one of the rocks, its tan scales marked with a black design as if imprinted with a paintbrush.

"What's that? Is it poisonous?"

Karim laughed. "A python, name python regius. I buy here but snake from West Africa. . Salesman tell me most popular pet snake in world. No danger.

It is non-ven, ven..." Karim fumbled for the word. "No poison."

"Oh, you mean non-venomous."

She walked back to the sofa and sat down, trying to mask her initial reaction to the python and pleased that vocabulary had always been one of her best subjects in school.

"Do you live here alone?"

"Of course."

"You must have many friends, then," she said, indicating the cups.

"Yes. Sofia, come and see all."

He took her hand and showed her the small kitchen and powder room, both impeccably neat and clean, and a guest bedroom with its own bathroom. He opened the door to a walk-in closet filled with a few clothes and eleven pairs of shoes arranged in rows. Finally he took her into his bedroom. She gasped. She'd only ever seen a waterbed on television and certainly not one as large as Karim's or with a casing of studded black leather. There was no bedding on it. A nearby black lacquer bench held three sets of white sheets, pillows, and two blankets. Next to the bench was a matching three-drawer desk holding a laptop and a laser printer.

On one long wall between two floor-two ceiling windows was a tall mahogany dresser with brass handles on its eight drawers. He opened them to display dozens of socks and underwear. The adjoining

87

walk-in closet was filled with designer suits, jackets, casual pants. A large shelf unit held dozens of shirts. She was surprised to see that several T-shirts were arranged neatly on hangers, and two large, bulging garment bags, their zippers closed, also hung on the rod. Additional built-in shelves were piled with underwear still in their packets, and socks next to a tie rack held several dozen silk ties. On hooks on the back wall of the closet were several baseball caps of different teams. A hardcover attaché case was on the floor.

"You like mostly dark colors," she said, feeling some of the suit and shirt fabrics, "except for your white suits. Do you have any of those long robes in those garment bags, the kind I've seen Arabs wear? What are they called?"

He frowned. "Sofia, I wear America clothes here."

At midnight Sofia arose as well as she could manage from the waterbed, laughing as it rocked and swayed beneath her and almost prevented her from stepping off and standing up.

"Karim, I have to go home. Anne will be worrying about me."

"Dear Sofia. Okay."

He went into the bathroom and she heard the shower running. Should she join him? He was her first. She had no idea what a lover's expectations were, especially not those of a foreigner. She decided to wait until he finished before taking a shower herself.

When they left the apartment Sofia was pleased he hadn't tried to persuade her to stay until morning or complained about getting up in the middle of the night to drive her home.

Parked at Anne's house Karim was as courteous as ever, opening the car door and walking her upstairs to the studio apartment. He kissed her on the cheek before leaving. Anne opened her eyes when Sofia got into bed next to her, then turned over, and went back to sleep.

"You came home really late, didn't you?" said Anne in the morning.

"I guess."

"Did you have a good time?"

Sofia only smiled in response and went into the tiny bathroom. No need to reveal my secret, she thought. I'm still getting used to being a real woman.

Chapter 18

The couple began spending most of their time together, shopping, going to the movies, and clubbing. When Sofia occasionally protested at their constant togetherness and reminded Karim that she needed to find a job he brushed off her concern. He reminded her he had plenty of money and pointed out that their shopping expeditions provided all she needed to wear, and that she enjoyed dining out a lot. It didn't occur to Sofia that, despite the streak of independence she had always shown, it was apparent it was no longer part of her personality. Her lover was in charge of almost every aspect of her life except her relationship with Anne. Yet, instead of feeling smothered she felt loved, cared for, and safe.

Nightclubs and strip joints were favorite venues that kept them out till the early hours. Before sunrise Karim took Sofia back to his bedroom and mid-morning he drove her to Anne's studio where she had the place to herself after Anne and Lorna left for work.

Shopping became a weekly activity when Karim took her to the finest boutiques and shoe stores, including Ferragamo. He insisted she wear the highest spiky heels they could find and dress in expensive designer outfits, instructing her to come out of the dressing rooms in clothes by Chanel, Yves San Laurent, Courreges, and Pucci to show him how they looked on her. If he said "No" she would try on something else until he was satisfied.

"We goofed around a lot at those times with me posing as a French model. Money seemed to be no problem. I felt I was living in an Arabian Nights fantasy."

Dazzled and showered with gifts Sofia nevertheless thought of herself as Miss No One From Nowhere. She still occasionally felt like a little girl from the sticks. Along with the designer clothes she managed to persuade Karim into buying her a couple of grunge outfits that were popular at the time with teenagers like Sofia such as stone-washed jeans and loose, homogenous plaid shirts. A few months later Karim would throw them out.

Sofia felt a little guilty for not following up on employment but ten days after meeting Karim all thoughts of her finding a job and a place of her own vanished.

"It became a ritual for us to end each date by going back to his house after a night out and then later return me to mine."

Soon, even that changed.

"We were having dinner at the Marrakesh, a Moroccan restaurant," Sofia told me, "when he suddenly reached across the table and grabbed my hand. He said, 'Sofia, you must come and live to me. Now. Tonight. I wish it.' Well, Victoria, you can imagine what a wonderful surprise it was to hear those words. I adored Karim and he made it clear he was in love with me. I wanted to spend the rest of my life with this exciting foreigner and his fascinating accent. I didn't hesitate. Looking back I believe I had been looking for a protector from the day my father left when I was eight. Of course I'll move in, I told Karim. Tomorrow. I knew Anne would give me an argument, Victoria, but I'd made up my mind."

In the morning Sofia pointed out to Karim that she needed some luggage to hold all the beautiful dresses and shoes he had bought her. He went into his closet and from a set of matching aluminum Gucci Rimowa luggage he selected two of the largest suitcases. He put them into the trunk of the car and drove Sofia to Anne's studio. Bursting with happiness, Sofia kept looking at Karim's profile as he drove, squeezing his shoulder until he brushed her hand off. At Anne's house he retrieved the suitcases from the trunk and set them on the sidewalk. He said he'd wait for her in the car.

Sofia took the suitcases up hoping to catch Anne before she left for work. She needed to break the news to her. Almost stumbling over the luggage in her hand Sofia called out her sister's name and rang the bell, too preoccupied to use her own door key. She burst in as soon as Anne opened the door and set the suitcases down.

"Sorry, I have my key but couldn't reach it. But I won't need it any more. Guess what? Karim has asked me to live with him." She twirled around in her excitement, her face flushed red and her eyes gleaming with joy. "Imagine that!"

"What? No, no. It's out of the question. You hardly know him. That's a crazy idea."

Stopped in her tracks, her face falling with disappointment at Anne's reaction, Sofia sat on the daybed staring up her.

"But I do know him. We've been together almost since our first date. You know him, too, and his friends. Why are you being so negative?"

"Honey, you are barely seventeen years old, much too young to be living with a guy. You're not even out of high school. It's only been four weeks since you left home. And you know I'm not too happy about all those clothes he bought you. Why can't you date him for a few months first?"

"Oh no, I love Karim. He loves me. He told me although it was strange the way he said it, halting, as if he had to push the words out but that's because hi English isn't good yet. . Well, he's an Arab. Besides, you know they're different to us. Anne, I know that Karim and I are meant to be together. I'm sorry but I am going. Please be happy for me, sis. Look at these beautiful suitcases he loaned me. They're the latest model. It's called Rimowa. Cool, right?" Her happiness was infectious and she saw that Anne was beginning to smile. "You'll come over a lot, won't you? Karim will cook his marvelous Middle Eastern dishes and we'll still double-date with you and Stefan."

Sofia went to the small closet that was now crammed with new clothes and shoes. She carefully folded and packed the skirts, dresses, blouses, suits, and jackets. With no space left for her several pairs of designer shoes she decided to hand-carry them separately in a plastic garbage bag she took from under Anne's kitchen sink, laughing to Anne that she'd make sure the fastidious Karim didn't see it.

"Why not?" said Anne. "Where's your duffel bag? You can put your shoes in that."

"Karim told me to throw it out. He said it was old and dirty and he didn't want it in his car. Can you imagine, he has a special suede drawstring bag for every pair of shoes. He's real fussy about stuff. I don't want him to know I have to use a plastic garbage bag."

"You said he's waiting downstairs for you. How can you hide it?"

"I'll come back for it later on the bus. He'll be at school all morning although he's been slacking off a lot lately. Don't worry, I have it all figured out. I know how he is. I'll make sure he's not home before I get back."

"But, Sofia, you shouldn't be starting a relationship where you have to sneak around."

"Oh, don't be silly. I'm not sneaking around. He gave me a door key." She took a keyring from her purse. "Look, isn't this neat? It has a miniature book on it." She held out the inch-long gold-etched cover of a tiny book attached to the keyring with seven gold links. "I don't know exactly what the book is, he said it's called the Koran which I think is their Bible. It's so cute."

"I have to go, honey, or I'll be late for work. Call me tomorrow or stop by. My break's still at two-thirty."

After Anne left Sofia finished packing and carried the suitcases, one at a time, downstairs, leaving the plastic bag of shoes for collection later. Karim was waiting at the curb, the trunk of the Buick open. Although physically small, he easily swung the heavy luggage inside then opened the passenger door for Sofia.

Her heart was beating fast with anticipation, picturing herself hanging up her clothes on the velvet hangers in Karim's walk-in closet and inserting each pair of shoes carefully into the shoe storage shelves alongside his own.

At the apartment Karim told her that her sweaters, underwear, and other items were to be arranged in separate drawers on the opposite side of the room.

"Sofia, keep belongings away to mine. Not touching. You take dresser there," he said, pointing to a four-drawer chest, "and must hang clothes at end. No touch."

Her mind swimming with excitement she didn't mind the odd instructions, figuring that Middle Easterners had their own rules. She had tried to look very matter-of-fact after Karim's surprising suggestion that she move in. Not only was she going to live with this man, she wouldn't have to look for a job. He'd made that clear, too. Best of all, they were in love with each other. She adored him. He often looked at her with affection, sometimes smiling at her faux pas moments when she made an obvious, often childish, mistake.

Her new home, she found, was like Grand Central Station in New York with students and men Karim said were his brothers and cousins, coming in and out from morning to mid-afternoon. Karim had told her his routine was to attend class from 7 a.m. to 3 p.m. but he never did so. He spent hours on the phone talking in Arabic. Cell phones were not in everyone's pocket in the early 1990s. Mobile phones were large, clumsy devices and often referred to as a "brick" back then. But quickly, by the mid-1990s their size had decreased drastically and their functions increased to become everyday tools. Karim kept a mobile phone in the kitchen, the living room, and in his bedroom. Sofia was free to use any of them whenever she wished.

"Karim made it clear right from the start," she said, "that he could never marry me and that we could not be together forever. He said he must marry the Muslin woman he'd been betrothed to since birth. What did I care, Victoria? I was 17 and enjoying life. Marriage was not on my agenda either."

When guests were at the house he never touched her and paid her little attention although he insisted they treat her respectfully, an unnecessary admonition as they barely acknowledged her presence ad never spoke to her. As soon as the men left and Karim was alone with Sofia his hands were all over her and he kept saying, "I love you."

She missed seeing Anne but was convinced her life was complete with only good times continuing forever. Never one to look ahead or plan into the future, Sofia remained impulsive although she failed to understand that the trait was greatly diminished as she fell under Karim's influence.

Chapter 19

At around the same time that Sofia met Karim in Portland, the leader of al Qaeda, Osama bin Laden, was in Sudan re-issuing a *fatwa*, a ruling on Islamic law that called for a *jihad*, a fight or holy war, against the United States, vowing to "cut off the head of the snake" as he regarded the Western Allies. Basking in relative peace after the short-lived Gulf War waged and won by the United States and 35 coalition forces, the country voted in Bill Clinton as president, and Disney released the movie, "Aladdin," destined to play a small but significant moment in Sofia's life with Karim.

Over the following days that stretched into weeks Sofia found herself part of the regular gatherings Karim held at their home on the river. Instead of being alone with her lover she found their living room constantly occupied by friends, guests, and visitors from abroad. Most of them were young, male, and well-dressed in designer jeans and top-of-the line expensive sneakers. Most of them smoked Turkish cigarettes. A few times an elderly man, bearded, burly, and dressed in a long ankle-length black robe, joined them and appeared to be a lecturer or teacher, He treated Sofia with great respect, much more so than the other men who, while obviously resenting her presence, would glance surreptitiously at her mini-skirted legs.

If there were late afternoon and evening meetings they sat at the dining table or on the floor around the elaborately-engraved brass Middle Eastern coffee table, covering the surface with blueprints and ordnance and street maps, as well as the dozens of photographs the students had taken during their outings. There were handwritten lists that they'd check off when matched with places and buildings. They talked, laughed, and at times held heated discussions, all in their own language.

They tried to appear mature, Sofia saw, but laughter gave them away when an obvious joke was shared and hand gestures added. She liked their infrequent camaraderie and pretended not to notice when their loud voices were heard throughout the apartment when they argued. Some of them had neatly trimmed beards, others preferred small goatees, but most, like Karim, were clean-shaven. She often hid a smile when any of the Arabs wore a baseball cap. It appeared to be a problem keeping it in place because of their thick, curly hair.

"What are they arguing about?" Sofia asked Karim the first time she joined the group, sitting in the chair near the window that Karim told her to occupy. She realized he didn't want her near his friends and their maps. Whenever she spoke, the

Arabs scowled at her.

"They argue of homework," said Karim. "School very difficult, and teachers no good."

"What's the problem with the teachers?"

"Too many ignorant. Please, Sofia, sit quiet. No questions. Say nothing."

It was continually clear to Sofia that her presence was not welcomed by the several friends, all of whom were Arabs. The men looked upon her with obvious contempt until they were admonished by their host to show her respect. Grudgingly, they complied with half-smiles and nods but they usually avoided meeting her eyes.

A few students traveled to Karim's house from Seattle where, he said proudly, there was a large Arab community. Although she didn't understand their language she picked up more than Karim realized. She was often able to figure out what they were discussing by their gestures, the marks they pointed to on the maps, and other signs. Sofia had excelled in languages at school and she was able to piece together far more than they knew. But she kept silent.

As the weeks went by the gatherings increased in size and were soon sorted into seven teams that Karim explained to Sofia were for the different classes and subjects they were taking at the two colleges, Lewis and Clark and Portland State University. Often two or three new young men joined the meetings and appeared shocked she was present. Some of them she never saw again. Later, she offered the opinion that they probably didn't make the cut that al Qaeda demanded from its operatives.

One time, after they left the house still talking raucously, she asked Karim if they all came from Saudi Arabia.

"Most, yes, and Yeminis. A few Persian Gulf Arabs from Kuwait, Qatar, Oman, Bahrain, Saudi Arabia, and the U.A.E. like my family. When I come to America my parents build new house, a gift from rich man in my country, Osama bin Laden."

It was a name she heard them speak often. She thought at first they were talking about the character in the movie, "Aladdin," one of her and Karim's favorite films. Karim laughed when she asked him about it and quickly corrected her but told her not to speak bin Laden's name in front of his friends, or to anyone else because he was a highly-placed man and needed to keep his name private in America.

"Karim told me that bin Laden was a very special, amazing person who they all revered," Sofia said at one of our recording sessions. "I was always curious about anything to do with Karim and I asked a lot of questions. He was happy to answer me, showing off at times, and I learned a lot about the Middle East. Karim was a militant Sunni and believed that the Shiites were ruining Islam. I understood hardly any of the religion side of it all and of course I kept my mouth shut. To me, they were all dorks."

At times, when Karim made derogatory remarks about America, Sofia sprang to her country's defense, pointing out its constitutional rights of free speech, and freedom of choice that he and his friends were enjoying here. Sofia and her lover also discussed freedom of religion which was often their main point of disagreement.

Karim's opinion was that all Christian religions in America were evil and that church members were fooled into believing that Jesus Christ was God's son. Sofia staunchly defended her beliefs although she didn't always practice them, and at those times Karim would smile condescendingly, and finally take her into his arms.

"I basked in his attention," she said. "All I wanted was to be with him morning, noon, and night. We'd go out in whichever car he was leasing and pick up a couple of his friends. We'd drive to kind of strange places and they did weird things like circling around the outside of the airport, or walk down to the riverbanks, and they always had their cameras and binoculars."

Sofia said that they went to the shopping mall parking lots without going inside. They took photos from the car. Everywhere they went they took photos. To her their cameras looked expensive and had a built-in flash which Karim told her proudly was the latest technology.

Twice they drove to meet with Abdullah al Thani whom she learned was the moneyman who supplied the men with cash and who always had a laptop with him. When Karim received his share of the money Sofia was sent to the bank to deposit it into his account.

At first, Karim asked Sofia to handle all of his cash transactions because he was unfamiliar with U.S. bank procedures and was unsure of his English. He said that the money came in from Germany and Saudi Arabia and if there were any questions at the bank she was to write them down and come back home so he could give her the answers. She pointed out that the bank manager could call him on the phone but Karim said no, that he wanted things done his way. He told Sofia how much money to withdraw each time and to be sure to bring back the receipts. When she was no longer asked to handle the chore she assumed he took it over himself.

"When I handled his finances I knew who the money men were, how the sums of money were transferred and through whom, and I knew which banks it all went to. I later gave all of this information to the FBI," she said. "Karim told me not to call the money guy by his full name, Abdullah al Thani, but refer to him as 'Uncle Abdullah.' We also met with Nasim Hassan who came and stayed with us, and the cultural attaché at the Saudi embassy often visited our home. Others I remember were Nasim's cousin from Qatar who Karim said was his mentor. There were many other Arabs I met from Saudi Arabia but their names are a blur."

Chapter 20

During their many outings the men shot hundreds of photos focusing on the Burnside and Morrison bridges and waiting for low tide so they go beneath to take measurements of the girth of each bridge's support structure. Puzzled by their bizarre behavior but following along at his heels Sofia asked Karim why they chose to photograph such boring sites as abutments under the bridges that spanned the river.

"We look if Uncle Abdullah's yacht go to pass underneath," she was told. The men heard him and snickered at each other so she assumed it wasn't true.

They also went to the Bonneville Dam and to the industrial areas around the city's international airport. When they took pictures of Portland's civic buildings they wrote everything down in notebooks. They loitered at the Trojan Nuclear Plant near Rainier, and watched news reports of its imminent closure.

Sofia went with them on all of their photo shoots although sometimes she was told to wait in the car at various destinations. Often she was surprised at their attention to detail such as counting how many planes flew into Sea-Tac airport over a period of an hour, and calculating the height of Portland's downtown skyscrapers and counting the number of floors in each. They photographed train tracks, river traffic that plied the Willamette River, and the old Portland City Hall building with its brown façade and architecture.

Three or four times they drove north to Seattle and parked in the harbor where they took photos of the port while she waited patiently in the car. They videotaped cargo ships. Around mid-afternoon on their first visit they drove to a scuba shop where two of them rented equipment and went scuba-diving. Later they photographed the Space Needle then drove to a downtown shopping mall to take more photos.

"After we had circled around it in the parking lot I got the impression they dismissed the mall as a target because Karim waved his hand as if pushing it away."

"Weren't you suspicious?" I asked.

"No, not then. Karim reminded me they were just engineering and architecture students who were studying how perfectly designed many American structures were, and how shops were arranged and situated in the malls. At our house they often watched videos of how buildings were planned and constructed. I was just as interested in watching them as they were."

105

Sofia turned to me as she repeated Karim's words of praise for the architects, her eyes glistening with tears.

"I'm so ashamed now but back then when he said things like that I felt proud and even patriotic to be an American, to realize that these worldly people from lands going back thousands of years would come here to appreciate what we, a young country, could teach them. Coming from their ancient cultures, well, it just blew me away."

Sofia's lover began leasing a new car every two or three months, switching from the latest luxury model to another whether European, Japanese or American.

"He was like a kid with a new toy each time," she said as she remembered going with him to the car dealerships. "There seemed to be no reason for making the changes. Maybe he was thinking he was fooling anyone who he thought might be following him, or perhaps he did it because he could, showing off to his Arab friends."

Money was obviously no deterrent.

"To my mind I was living in a fantasy, a soap opera," said Sofia. "He loved buying things for both of us and walked around with wads of cash. He was obviously proud to show me off and when we went to the clubs he bought me glittery cocktail dresses and evening gowns to wear. Not a lot of jewelry was coming my way but he spent a lot on himself with gold bracelets, two watches, silver and gold tiepins, and a gold chain holding a pendant engraved with Arabic words "

Bemused at their eagerness to soak up the American way of life, especially with their passion for fast food, flashy cars, and clubs where they drank vast amounts of liquor, Sofia at first attributed the activities to their curiosity about Western culture and their eagerness to savor those aspects of American culture, most of it prohibited in their own countries.

"I didn't care what they did as long as I was with Karim," Sofia told me. "Their actions didn't seem sinister. His friends always grumbled about me coming along on their trips but he took no notice. It was as if he couldn't shake off his love for me, and it was obvious that as he was the leader of the group, the others were obedient, accepting what appeared to be his orders without argument although the men often argued among themselves. What an impressionable fool I was," she said bitterly.

At times it seemed the Arabs were disorganized and lacked direction yet Sofia could see they shared a unity, giving Sofia a first-hand look, as she later described it, of the creation of a terrorist cell. She watched as it was structured, how the men were sorted into groups, and who was in command. It appeared to Sofia that they were comprised of four inner cells; a fifth group were errand boys; group six were all from the U.A.E. and those in group seven were engineers.

Karim passed around catalogs of which laptop computers each man was to buy and gave them brochures of cars they were to lease on short-term contracts, or purchase. He told them how often to turn the leases over, warned them to drive at the posted speed limit in order not to be stopped by the police, and never to drive drunk.

Over the following several weeks Sofia met more and more young Arabs at gatherings in the home she shared with Karim and she still questioned their odd photo sessions. How many photos did they need? She went with Karim when he drove to other apartments, telling his passengers to write down their addresses which later she found turned out to be safe houses. But after a while she became bored and disinterested in accompanying them and preferred to stay home and watch her favorite soap operas on television.

"I loved 'The Young and the Restless,' and 'The Bold and the Beautiful,'" she told me. "I identified with the female characters, and wept and laughed at the dramas that enveloped them. Karim called me a silly teenager but I really loved those shows."

When he wasn't buying triple-cheese pizzas Karim, who enjoyed cooking his own native dishes, took her to the Middle Eastern markets and bazaars in Portland to buy halal meats, tahini, kebabs, and spices.

"It was fascinating walking through the food stalls," said Sofia. "We stocked up on cloves, pine nuts, yogurt, mountains of spinach, and hummus. Karim bought fava beans, tomatoes, garlic and lemons to make a vegan breakfast, and our favorite, the dainty Turkish delight sweets loaded with dates. Our apartment smelled great, too, because Karim always kept jasmine burning as incense."

At the market she didn't notice too many men wearing the keffiyeh, the checkered Arab headdress secured around the head with a ring, she told me, but a few women were swathed in the traditional long black dress that covered them from head to toe. Karim told Sofia it was called a burka.

"Mostly, though, the Middle Eastern women that were shopping at the markets wore Western clothes and hijab headscarf. They looked so exotic. I wanted to wear one, too, but Karim was appalled at my suggestion. He was so prissy sometimes. I just shrugged it off."

The couple enjoyed exploring each other's lifestyles, discussing their religions' beliefs and practices. Karim told Sofia of his background, of growing up in the United Arab Emirates, and Sofia responded by describing her own childhood. They found they had a lot more in common than they realized when they talked about their mothers and fathers, and compared their lives with their siblings.

She was intrigued by tales of his background, of Ramadan, and other Middle Eastern customs. They shared how their religious doctrines impacted their upbringing and how great it was to be free of those restrictions, his Islam, hers Jehovah's Witness. Although Karim was the more conservative of the two, together they indulged in the forbidden twin temptations of alcohol and cigarettes, and continued to enjoy going to strip clubs and dancing till dawn. When the other Arabs visited Karim they often watched the rented porno videos after their "homework" was finished for the day.

"We were both living without parental or religious supervision and we went crazy. We were like kids released from school and totally in sync with each other. We found that initially our strongest bond centered on music and after that, the movies. We went to the video stores almost every day, practically living at Blockbuster," said Sofia. "Karin rented a lot of action movies. He loved anything that starred Arnold Schwarzenegger. We were both avid Hollywood fans. Karim loved going to see the latest films. He was partial to the Bruce Lee martial arts action movies, studying his technique, and renting karate and judo videos. I teased him but I was really impressed with the concentration he brought to trying to perfect the martial arts training routines. He'd jump on and off the sofa to copy Jean-Claude Van Damme's moves."

They shared a love of pop music, and had their special song, Whitney Houston's "I'll Always Love You." Karim was infatuated with anything of the

Rolling Stones. They assured each other they were in love, and from the way Karim made love to her, his tenderness and his loving ways, Sofia was convinced of his feelings for her. His tenderness, however, didn't translate into a love for pets except for his python. Sofia suggested several times that they adopt a rescue dog or cat as she often did in Dundee. The Front Street apartment management allowed small dogs but Karim laughed and said only if she found one little enough to feed his snake, a remark that sent shivers down Sofia's back.

Chapter 21

The number of Arabs visiting the house began yet again to increase and Sofia tired even more of them being always around not only at the house to play cards and have meetings but also at the restaurants and nightclubs. They'd show up at the same movie theaters; they all went bowling together, and played billiards. The only time she had Karim completely to herself was at night on the black leather waterbed which Sofia found so uncomfortable. Even there, Karim had rules. He didn't make the bed with sheets and pillows until he and Sofia were ready to retire.

In the mornings, no matter what time they went to bed, they arose at 6:30 a.m. so that he could strip the sheets and launder them, his daily ritual. He took a half-hour shower, shampooed his hair every day, rubbed pricey lotion all over his body, and never wore the same clothes twice without taking them to the dry cleaners. Only when he was dressed did he make breakfast for them both, consisting mostly of pita bread, hummus with jam, and dahl. Three times a week Karim made scrambled eggs sprinkled with herbs.

Sofia was intrigued with her lover's coffee ritual. He had brought his traditional ornate coffee pot with him from Saudi Arabia, a gift from his mother. He always prepared and served it the same way, brewing enough to last throughout day. First, he would set the pot of water on the stove and bring it to a boil. He'd add two tablespoons of Turkish coffee and lower the heat, turning it off after five minutes. Then he added three tablespoons of ground carda-mom and a one-quarter teaspoon of saffron.

Next, Karim picked up the pot in his left hand although she knew he was right-handed, and filled a small hand-painted ceramic coffee cup only half-way. He'd push it towards her with his right hand. She noticed the cup had no handle and asked him why. He declined to answer and instead told her not to drink it too quickly. She later learned that using the left hand to deliver something was considered bad manners by Middle Easterners and that if a cup was filled to the rim it meant that the server wants the recipient to drink up quickly and depart.

"That coffee was the best I'd ever tasted," Sofia told me. "I asked what the aroma was and he said the coffee often included spices that I told him I'd never heard of nor tasted before."

After their leisurely breakfast the couple usually set out for Barbur World Food market to shop for coriander, cloves, and other spices, and visit the butcher. She noticed that even though Karim claimed the food he bought at the market's small grocery stores and specialty shops was cooked according to the Koran, he continued to enjoy many American dishes when they dined out that were forbidden by his faith.

Other stores were n their agenda, almost weekly. "Karim loved buying me clothes and took me to the best shops. He was amazed at the variety of designs and fabrics from all over the world, and particularly loved Italian shoes."

He didn't neglect himself and picked out silk shirts and elegant suits that draped well over his lean frame. His European designer sweaters were so costly Sofia wondered if the money-well was bottomless. None of the Arabs who frequented Karim's apartment were as well turned out nor as clothes-conscious as Karim and occasionally they teased him for the formal attire that he preferred wearing in contrast to their jeans, albeit expensive, their sweatshirts, and Versace studded-denim jackets.

"When he leased a car every three months he was like a kid with a new toy each time," Sofia said as she remembered going with him to the car dealerships. "There seemed to be no reason for making the changes so frequently. Maybe he was thinking he was fooling anyone who he thought might be following him, an issue I didn't understand until much later, or perhaps he leased the fancy cars because he could, showing off to his friends. Money was obviously no deterrent. It came rolling in to his bank regularly."

In her opinion, she said, she was living in a fantasy, a soap opera.

"He loved buying things for both of us and walked around with wads of cash. He was obviously proud to show me off. He bought me glittery cocktail dresses and evening gowns to wear when we went to the clubs. Not a lot of jewelry was coming my way but he spent a lot on himself with gold bracelets, two watches, silver and gold tiepins, and a gold chain holding a pendant engraved in Arabic."

Occasionally he bought several items of men's clothing in various sizes that Sofia noticed were never hung in his closet. Where did they go? Who were they for?

Chapter 22

Two months after her daughter moved in with Karim and listening to Sofia's excited phone calls about her life with him, Erika made plans to visit, bringing along young Jeff. Alarmed by what sounded to her as a very strange household she wanted to judge for herself the situation that her teenage daughter had recklessly flung herself into. She was worried by the stories Sofia related with great excitement about her life with the Arabs. Had Sofia's high intelligence deserted her? If only she'd gone to college on a scholarship instead of running away from home, Erika reflected.

Sofia's mother arrived at the Front Avenue apartment prepared to persuade her daughter to come back home to Dundee, an uphill battle, she conceded, but worth a try. She soon realized that nothing could be further from Sofia's mind, that her daughter was entranced by Karim's different way of life, his foreignness. Erika was far less enamored with her daughter's choice of lover and the money he lavished on her. She'd already become suspicious of the strange activities Sofia told her about weeks earlier. It was her fears about the man that impelled her to pay a visit to her daughter's new home. Erika did, however, approve of the location when she rang the bell of the two-bedroom apartment in the complex on the east bank of the Willamette River.

Sofia opened the door and greeted her mother and brother with hugs, explaining that Karim was out but would be back shortly. She bubbled over with enthusiasm, raving about the man she was living with, saying that he adored her.

"He buys me anything I want. Wait till you see my closet."

When Karim arrived a few minutes later Erika's first impressions of him were of elegance, wealth, and power as he came strolling through the front door carrying a huge bouquet of red and yellow roses. Wearing a dark gray silk suit, that Erika, with her tailoring background estimated to have cost a small fortune, he presented the flowers to her with a flourish. She knew he was only twenty-two years old but his aura of sophistication was that of a world-travelled cosmopolitan.

After Erika and Jeff settled their luggage into the guest bedroom Sofia took them into the living room for coffee where Karim was already seated in one of the black leather armchairs. Erika tried to engage him in conversation about his family and his country but he brushed her questions off with a flip of the hand, claiming they were just ordinary people, and that Saudi Arabia was like most other Middle Eastern countries. His evasions didn't sit well with Erika but Jeff was far more easily satisfied, finding Playboy and Ebony magazines under the sofa. That night he sneaked them into the bathroom to read after assuring himself that his mother was asleep.

Karim's friends mostly stayed away during Sofia's family visits but within an hour of their leaving to drive back to Dundee, his two brothers, Hassan and Zafir along with three friends were knocking at the front door. By now Sofia had picked up a several words of greeting and used them whenever Karim had visitors – always male Arabs – but they never responded in kind. She was ignored, as usual, as they brushed by her.

"I didn't care. I was learning so much about foreigners and how they lived," she said. "I didn't understand much when Karim and his friends talked but I was gradually getting a sense of the meaning. I barely noticed that I didn't see Anne any more, or that I had no friends of my own. It didn't matter. I was so completely besotted with Karim I thought of nothing else. What a gullible fool I was."

Sofia observed that aside from the affection he showed her and his fervent lovemaking, the most emotion he showed was when he called his parents, Bathshar and Saidah. Often teary-eyed when they spoke, Karim explained his mood to Sofia afterwards by saying he was very homesick and had asked his father when he could come back. He must stay in America, he was told.

"Karim would sit on the sofa waiting for the overseas connection to go through. When he cried too much to speak he would hand the phone to me. His father spoke quite good English and always said kind words to me. He knew I was nowhere near as well-educated as his son, and that I came from a family in a small, rural town."

One day Karim told Sofia that his parents had come into a lot of money and were building a big new house in Al-Ain, a university town on the border with Oman. She later speculated that the finances came from al Qaeda and were filtered through a bank in another country in appreciation of their son's activities in America. The "activities" that she later found out were so deadly.

Chapter 23

"I came to Portland with an open mind," Erika recounted to me. "But for some reason my intuition told me not to trust Karim. He was polite, smooth, and appeared wealthy. He was a clean-shaven young man, nice-looking, and well-groomed. He welcomed Jeff, my youngest son, and me with a handshake. It was not a good, firm shake but brief and limp." Erika laughed at the memory. "For Sofia's sake I wanted to like him and I knew that if I was to question their lifestyle she would cut me off. With all of my children my motto was the more support you give them, the easier it is for them to listen to you when things go wrong."

Erika was impressed with the apartment, its elegant furnishings, the location overlooking the river, and admired the bong pipe in one corner of the room. It was ornate with gold fittings for the hoses, and the glass was clouded with a violet tint. Sofia told her mother that the color was a result of the smoke. She said the bong was a gift from his father. It was obvious that marijuana was smoked in it by the smell.

"The house reeked of it," Jeff said.

When Erika remarked on the beauty of the small midnight-blue and black velvet prayer rug on the arm of the sofa Karim became agitated and asked her not to touch it. Rectangular in shape, exquisitely embroidered with illustrations of arches and pillars, the mat was embossed with a tall black minaret in the center of the design. He told Erika that he prayed five times a day in his bedroom. Sofia, though, told her mother privately that it wasn't true and that he kept the prayer rug stuffed behind one of the large sofa pillows if no Arabs were expected to visit. When there were meetings Karim took the rug out, folded it once as per tradition, and ostentatiously draped it across the back of an armchair.

"He's not as religious as he wants you to believe," Sofia said when Erika repeated how beautiful she thought the rug was. "He never goes to a mosque, as far as I know."

"Doesn't it bother you that he lies?"

"Oh no, it's just his way.

"Honey, I wish you weren't so impressionable. You should have given more thought to moving in with him. These meetings with students, they seem strange, not like study sessions from what you tell me."

"Mom, he's so good to me. Yes, he likes his own way but it really is okay, it's fine with me."

Young Jeff liked Karim when they first met although he admitted later he never got a good vibe from him.

"He was short, about the same height as my sister, even a little shorter, but he had a totally different air about him, like he thought of himself as someone special. He wore expensive clothes and used a wonderful-smelling cologne. When we went out to a foreign restaurant for dinner he ordered all kinds of exotic dishes that I'd never heard of or seen before. It was exciting. Sofia told us that Karim was something to do with the prime minister of his country. She was really proud of him."

Sofia realized that her mother was concerned for her and needed to know she was safe in her new environment. For all her understanding of the reason for the three-day visit it became somewhat tense. Erika's suspicions mounted by the day when, one morning, Arab after Arab walked through the front door as if they owned the place and settled themselves in the living room. Often, they would hold only a brief conversation with Karim before leaving.

"Who are all these people? What are they doing here?"

"Oh, just students. They need Karim's advice, he's the smartest one of them all."

At times two of the men, always the same ones during Erika's visit, appeared to remonstrate and argue with Karim but he never lost his temper or shouted. He explained to Erika he had many friends and relatives visiting from his country and the students came to him for help with their homework as he now spoke English better than they did. To Erika it was plain Karim was the leader of something but what? Her suspicions grew as she observed the men bringing maps and spreading them out. She took Sofia's explanation of them as architecture students with a mountain of salt. At Karim's request she watched from the patio where she, Jeff and Sofia sat on the outdoor chairs each time Karim played host to his friends.

"They were respectful and friendly but seemed annoyed I was there," Erika told me. "Karim pointed out that one of them was the son of the Emir of Qatar and like the others was a student at Portland State University. If Sofia, Jeff and I were in the living room they'd go out onto the deck overlooking the river and continue their discussions. I did some research on relationships between men and women in the Arab world and their culture. While several countries like Egypt, Tunisia, Jordan and a few others have moved into the 20th century, many have not. I was interested to learn, too, Victoria, that female students are better at science and math than their male counterparts. Maybe in the coming century women will have more equality there."

Erika was relieved to see that her daughter appeared relatively as happy and in the same good spirits as she'd been in at high school although somewhat quieter. She reminded herself that although Sofia was still a kid at 18 years old she was maturing. Erika also noticed that Karim was controlling although Sofia didn't appear to realize it and didn't object to his orders that he often snapped out at her.

During the visit Erika mentioned that one afternoon she, Jeff, and Sofia were going to attend an afternoon session of a Circuit Assembly of the Jehovah's Witness. She expected Karin to object to Sofia joining them and prepared herself for an argument. To her shock Karim said he'd like to join them and asked what the service would consist of and how long it would last.

"Usually around three hours," Erika said she told him. "We begin with music and songs and people can talk about their recent experiences. Then there's a symposium and more talks and announcements. We finish up with a song and a prayer."

"Good. I come," said Karim. "Yes, okay?"

"Of course," said Erika.

She couldn't help wondering if he was afraid he'd lose control over her daughter if she was out of his sight or if he simply wanted to ingratiate himself with the family by attending their service. At the Assembly Erika noticed him observing the congregation and listening intently after the service began.

She was still uncomfortable, however, with her daughter's living arrangement. Her religion disapproved of unmarried couples living together; on the other hand she didn't want to see the relationship between Sofia and Karim result in marriage, so she was willing to accept the compromise although Sofia told her mother she was sure Karim would propose soon.

After admiring the sumptuous settee and armchairs, the high-end furniture, the touches of Middle Eastern artifacts, and art on the walls, Erika was taken aback by the python when Karim draped it around his neck like a shawl. When driving he put the snake in a large cloth bag, tied with a drawstring, and took it along with them when they went shopping and dining although he always left it in its bag inside the car when they reached their destination. Jeff remembers one instance well.

"The first evening when we went out for dinner Karim took the snake off his shoulders after he parked and stuffed it into this bag which he left on the front seat," Jeff said. "When we got back to the car and Karim opened the passenger door to get the snake, the bag was on the floor, open and empty. That meant the python could be anywhere in the car. Mom had already opened the back passenger door and sat down."

When Jeff asked what happened to the snake because the bag was empty Erika jumped out of the car quickly. "We searched high and low." he said,

"My mom was scared to think it could be roaming around the back seat. I reminded her it wasn't poisonous. I liked the snake and asked Karim if I could hang it around my neck, too, when we found it. Mom, of course, said no."

The reptile was finally discovered curled up in a corner of the Buick's trunk that could be accessed from openings behind the back seats. Karim grabbed the python and returned it to its bag. Back home he slid the snake back into the fish tank. Scowling, he then went out to the patio where he spent almost an hour on the telephone. Sofia took her mother into the kitchen to choose some spices to take home with her, including coriander, saffron, dried lemons, curry powders, and other seasonings.

The second evening of Erika and Jeff's visit Karim cooked dinner, the exotic smells of curry wafting through the entire apartment. Seven guests arrived, all Arab men. Although it was now common practice for Sofia, her mother was surprised at the unusual manner of dining. Instead of sitting at a table as they did for breakfast and lunch, Karim spread newspapers over the large coffee table in the living room, then covered them with aluminum foil. There were several different dishes in bowls which Karim upended into separate piles directly onto the foil. Only Erika used a fork and sat in a chair after filling a plate with food; the others ate with their fingers, digging deep into the chicken and lamb curry, Basmati rice, cucumbers, sour cream, pita bread, and fresh fruit.

"Jeff was in his element," Sofia told me laughing, "breaking all kinds of Mom's etiquette rules."

"It was really excellent food," said Erika. "The curry in particular was delicious, the meat falling apart. When we'd had our fill Karim picked up the edges of the newspapers, wrapped them around the remaining food, and threw them way. They never kept any leftovers."

Before Erika left to return to Dundee Karim insisted that she accept his bank check for $2,000. Puzzled as to the reason for the money she nevertheless took it in order to avoid an argument but she never cashed it. Later, she would give it to the FBI. At her house the agents also confiscated a Koran, the sacred text that Erika was given by Anne's new boyfriend, Fadid who, oddly, inserted his own photo into the book. The FBI didn't return the items, not that Erika wanted them back, but she wondered if the agents thought that Fadid was part of the 9/11 planning.he likes his own way but it's okay, it's fine with me."

Chapter 24

Erika went home with many misgivings. Her daughter appeared to have no friends of her own and it seemed she was cut off from her sister, Anne, as Sofia said she hadn't seen her in a long time.

"Why not?" Erika said.

"Oh, Karim and I are always so busy and when he has the students over he doesn't want me to leave the house."

"Why is that?"

"He doesn't want me driving his car, and he feels it's not safe on the buses."

"That's ridiculous. There are no crimes on Portland's buses."

"Well, I like staying with him, anyway. It's okay, Mom, I'll call Anne soon."

Erika was forced to acknowledge to herself that her previously high-spirited, headstrong daughter had succumbed to Karim's every demand, dressing in the clothes he told her to wear, listening to his choice of music on the car radio and on the record player, and obeying when he told her how to fix her hair. She accepted his orders without complaint, leaving Erika much more worried about her daughter's future than when she arrived.

"When Karim leaves the house, Sofia told her mother, "I play my own kind of music, mostly Nirvana and Pearl Jam. I know the lyrics to every top 1992 song."

Erika realized that her daughter was still a typical teen focused on fashion, rock bands, and dancing, reminding herself that Sofia was only 17 years old, and regretting she had fallen for a foreigner whose behavior and activities disturbed her.

Young Jeff, on the other hand, had a grand time during the visit and hoped they could go back there soon. He had found more porno magazines under Karim's bed and although he knew he'd never be allowed to watch them there were also half a dozen porno movies whose cover illustrations were exciting to the young boy.

The visit ended with tears from mother and daughter and a request.

"Please, Sofia, will you come to Dundee for a few days?" said Erika. "I will come and pick you up."

"Oh, no. Karim needs me here."

Chapter 25

"Another Wainwright family visit was in the offing. Her brother, Alan, asked if he, his wife, Cynthia, and baby Gerald could stay with her and Karim for a couple of days while he was in Portland on business for his insurance company. Sofia gladly acquiesced as she had never met Alan's family. She called Anne, their first contact in months, to give her the news. Anne told her that their brother was concerned after Erika told him about her living arrangements.

"Oh, so it's another family member coming here to check me out?"

"We're all concerned that you have isolated yourself from us," said Anne. "I haven't seen you myself in months."

"It's just that we're busy, that's all."

"Everyone's busy, Sofia. But I'm you sister and can easily come over there for a visit. You just haven't invited me, and you sure as heck haven't come over here. You know you are always welcome, and so is Karim. We should have a double date like we used to."

"Oh, Karim is tied up with all his relatives who come over from Saudi Arabia. They usually stay with us and we are constantly going grocery shopping. It's often a madhouse here."

"I sure hope it calms down when Alan and Cynthia come to visit. Can you accommodate little Gerald?"

"Sure. I asked Alan and he said that the baby is almost three years old and can sleep with him and Cynthia."

"Sis, after Alan leaves why don't you come here for a few days? We can catch up with each other's lives. I'm due for some days off."

"You don't understand. I am needed here."

Anne let the matter drop. She knew her sister too well not to continue to pursue the issue.

"When are they coming?"

"In two days. I'm already excited."

Alan and his family's mid-morning arrival at the apartment was warmly greeted by Sofia and less so by Karim and another Arab that Alan was told now lived with them, a cousin from Saudi Arabia. There were also three other men present whom Sofia said were students at Portland State University. Sofia explained that they came over to the house almost every day to study together.

"It was a fall weekday morning when students are usually in class," Alan told Erika later, "They all arrived with identical black briefcases rather than backpacks or satchels that students usually carry their books in. I was surprised that there were no text books or any kind of books around although they did bring out notebooks. Then, as soon as they realized Karim had company they put the notebooks back into their briefcases and left."

Alan glanced at a pile of pornographic movies on the coffee table and their colorful covers displaying naked men and women in sexual poses. Karim, seeing his glance, quickly picked them up and carried them into another room, then Alan heard him on the phone in the kitchen ordering several large pizzas, impressed with Karim's command of English. Alan assumed the so-called students would be staying for lunch. He was correct. Three more Arabs came into the apartment at 12:30 p.m. and settled into the living room, obviously well familiar with their surroundings.

"I listened to them speak in their own language," Alan related to me on my tape recorder. "They took no notice of me, Cynthia, or Gerald, which I thought was strange. There was no interest at all in me nor did they ask what business I was in. I found it weird because normally foreigners and tourists are curious about our country and want to know about Americans, where we live and work and what we do for a living. One thing was obvious, I could see that they all loved pizza. Sofia told me they had it almost every day."

When the students left they took Karim's cousin with them so that Alan's family could sleep in his bedroom. That evening Karim cooked and they ate on the terrace overlooking the river watching the boat traffic go by. Alan also reported back to Erika that everything in the household appeared calm and the relationship between his sister and her boyfriend was agreeable.

On the day Alan and his family packed up to leave, a Thursday, Sofia begged them to stay a few days longer.

"Come on, it's almost the weekend. Surely your boss would understand if you take Friday off."

"Thanks, but we really do have to get back," Cynthia said in the parking lot as she strapped Gerald into the child's safety car seat. "A neighbor is watching our dogs and we have things to do at home before the workweek starts."

"Yes. You must go," said Karim.

Sofia and Alan looked at each other, almost laughing as they realized Karim was totally unaware of the effect and intent of his words.

"He didn't mean it that way," Sofia quickly said with a nervous giggle. "He's still learning English even though Alan thinks he's almost fluent. Karim has no idea how his choice of words sound sometimes."

Karim turned at her words, spat out a phrase in Arabic that sounded like a curse, and went back into the house. Sofia shrugged, aware she had embarrassed him. After a hasty goodbye to Alan and his family she followed Karim inside. She knew she was in for a furious scolding.

A month later more visitors arrived, Yasin ben Halim and a man he said was his brother. They stayed for two days, sleeping on the sofa and having long discussions with Karim. After they left Sofia was curious about the visit and to her delight Karim was in a talkative mood.

"Yasin tell me stop nightclubbing," Karim said with a grin. "He think too much attention to ourselves. Also, careful for spending money, and with bank, and stop shopping."

"Really? No nightclubs? He means you, not me. You rarely take me anymore, even to the dance clubs."

More and more frequently Karim went out at night without Sofia. His excuse was that his friends needed to meet him at a restaurant for dinner but afterwards they wanted to go clubbing. Sofia was jealous but not too worried because he never stayed out all night.

"Also, Yasin say no strip place."

"What does he mean by that? No one cares how many clubs we go to except me when you go out with your friends at night and leave me home."

"He also tell me to break attachment to you."

"What? This isn't an attachment. Didn't you tell him we're deeply in love?"

Karim raised his shoulders in a shrug and said nothing.

"I'm glad he told you to stay home more."

The admonitions had no effect on Karim as Sofia was to learn the next day.

Chapter 26

"Come to police station. Bring many money from safe. Now. Be quick. Take taxi."

Awakened at 4 a.m. by the telephone Sofia listened to Karim shouting, for once, at the top of his voice.

"Which police station? Are you all right? What has happened?"

She heard Karim ask for the address.

"Central Precinct," he said into the phone. "Second Avenue. Come. Now."

"Are you injured? Tell me what's happened."

"Not injured. Hurry."

Sofia dressed hastily, called for a cab, took a large envelope from Karim's desk drawer and filled it with several bundles of $100 bills from the safe. When the taxi arrived she gave the driver the address and urged him to drive as fast as possible, that her husband might be ill. With no details from Karim she was left to speculate during the short drive. What would cause the police to bring Karim to the station? Had he and his friends run over someone? He wasn't a violent person, not even when he flew into one of his rare rages but she couldn't say the same for his companions. Was it a hit-and-run? She had watched the three of them leave the house the apartment that night after Karim told her they were having dinner with a very important person from Saudi Arabia.

"Here we are, miss." The driver broke into her thought as he pulled over to the curb. "Shall I wait?"

"Yes, you'd better, I'm not sure where my friend's car is."

Inside the precinct arguments raged back and forth between all parties. The Arabs, the police, and a screaming blonde nearby. Sofia finally grasped the fact that the men were accused of rape by the woman.

"Rape? That's ridiculous," she said. "They don't need to rape anyone. They have plenty of girlfriends."

The men denied a rape occurred. The cops appeared to believe them because they knew the woman as having alleged other men raped her over the years. Her credibility was in doubt. But the charge of drunkenness remained although by now the men had almost sobered up.

Sofia talked with the cops, asking for an explanation of the entire episode. The police said they had stopped Karim when another driver called 911 and reported a Mercedes-Benz wandering all over the road and into the other lanes. When police caught up with them and pulled them over the men and the woman were handcuffed and taken to the precinct where she claimed they raped her.

One of the detectives, David O'Neill, talked to Sofia about the charges and introduced her to a bail bondsman, to whom she paid $5,000 for Karim's release. An arraignment would take place at a later date. Sofia, finding O'Neill sympathetic, told him of her relationship with Karim and the Arabs living with them, and confiding that she expected to marry him soon. The detective advised her to split from her current situation and urged her to go back home to Dundee. He was fatherly, but, as Sofia told me later, there was no way she was about to take his advice.

Each of the detainees had been allowed a phone call. One of them talked to someone at the Saudi embassy while Karim called a lawyer he knew, one that had been recommended by the embassy a year earlier when. Karim had been involved in a car crash and needed legal representation.

Within an hour an emissary from the Saudi Arabian embassy appeared at the jail to pay the bail bondsman for the two other Arabs, after having been advised that Karim had already paid. After further discussions they were allowed to leave two hours later, and returned home in a taxi, Sofia having paid off the previous driver. Karim was told his car had been impounded and given a number to call for retrieval information. Back at the apartment the two visitors went to their bedroom without saying a word but Sofia didn't let Karim off so lightly.

"I screamed at him for hours," she told me. "I was furious. He kept saying the others raped the woman. We finally went to bed after Karim took a shower. I heard the others taking one, too, in their bathroom."

Still jealous and angry Sofia went through scenarios in her head, with back-and-forth mental arguments about the arrest. She was inclined to believe Karim didn't rape the prostitute because of his fastidious nature and because the woman said it happened, if she was telling the truth, in the back seat while Karim was driving. However, the fact remained the police had hauled all of them into the station. Had he pulled off the road somewhere so that the he could also rape the woman? Sofia barely slept that night with doubts flooding her mind and her lover turned away from her and appearing to be in a deep sleep.

"The next morning," said Sofia, "we didn't speak. Karim made coffee and breakfast as usual, though, and called Abdullah. They had a long conversation, little of which I understood, of course, except for his name."

After the call Karim, in a morose mood, paced around for a while then abruptly left with the others and they drove off. As usual he didn't tell her where they were going, and as usual she accepted the situation. Had it been evening she would have assumed that he was either going to a strip club or meeting someone he was having an affair with.

That afternoon, after returning from another outing, this one brief, the others went onto the patio, leaving Sofia to experience one of the biggest surprises of her life. Karim appeared flustered and she could tell from his expression that there was anger beneath the surface.

"What's wrong?" she asked as soon as he came back into the living room through the patio door.

"We marry." Karim's face was grim. Was this a marriage proposal? He looked extremely unhappy.

"Has something happened? What did you say? Marry?"

"I meet Uncle Abdullah. No more questions."

"Well, do you want to hear my answer? I guess this is for a real. My answer is yes. Yes!" She tried to embrace him but he pushed her away.

"We go for quick wedding."

"Karim, I am so, so thrilled. But first my mom has to make my wedding dress. I know exactly the design I want. I've been drawing sketches of it since high school. We may have to order the lace I want if it's not available locally and..."

Her words trailed off as he turned away and went into the kitchen. Sofia followed him.

"Karim, aren't you happy to get married?"

As usual ignoring her question he said, "Next week we move to different apartment."

"Where? And why?"

"More cousins and uncle coming. We go to Lake Oswego. Three bedrooms."

A suburb of Portland and eight miles south of the city, One Jefferson Parkway at Lake Oswego was one of the most affluent apartment communities outside the city. Flowers and fountains greeted visitors at the entrance to the complex. Several famous pro basketball, baseball and NFL football players were residents, and, ironically in light of later events, a handful of retired U.S. Chiefs of Staff, and corporate CEOs. Access to the lake was private and for residents only, as were the golf course and other sports amenities within its confines.

For the move to the new apartment Karim hired a truck and two handymen to transport his and Sofia's clothes and shoes and other personal belongings. He also took the fish tank and its occupant, the python, the bong pipe, the prayer rug, the brass coffee table, the coffee pot, a few other pieces of kitchenware, and everything in the pantry.

"Why aren't we taking the furniture?"

"No, we leave it here. More relatives coming. I rent furniture for other apartment at Lake Oswego.

"You said that our new place is a three-bedroom so does that mean some people will stay with us there, too?"

"Go and pack dresses."

Karim rented three more single beds for the two guest rooms, making it a total of five beds, and busied himself placing everything in the correct order. The furniture was more luxurious than his previous rentals and included a large tan leather sectional sofa, four matching armchairs, bookshelves, and a desk that he placed in the master bedroom. The modern glass dining table and chairs could seat ten people although they still sat on the floor most of the time to eat. He rented floor lamps for the living room and bedroom, and small bedside lamps for the guest rooms. He asked the rental company to supply enough dinnerware and silverware for eight people, and different sized pots and pans.

When Sofia asked again exactly how many relatives would be living with them he shrugged, his usual response when he didn't want to reply. She asked if they were students.

"Yes, yes," he answered irritably.

"Are any of the students or visitors women?" she said.

"Of course not." He looked appalled at the question.

Why hadn't any women such as sisters or wives come to visit, she wondered although she was aware of their culture. Sofia understood Karim's initial explanation that it was their custom for women not to travel outside their country but she had talked to a few Arabian women at the Middle Eastern markets in downtown Portland and they spoke with heavy accents so she knew they were not American-born. Again, his reply didn't hold water.

Sofia was impressed with her new home and happily helped Karim arrange the furniture. She set up the kitchen, lined the cabinets throughout the apartment after Karim took her to a hardware store for shelf paper, and made the beds for the expected boarders who would be living with them. It took three days before Karim was satisfied with everything and the couple were able to take a break. But Sofia's mind was focused on her upcoming life-changing event.

"Karim, I want to talk about our wedding. Are we having a reception? I need to get invitations printed up and sent to my family and friends. How many people are you inviting? Have you made a list of your guests? Will your parents come over from Saudi Arabia?"

"No."

"Karim, there's something wrong, I can feel it. Tell me what's going on."

"I must marry because of police arrest. Maybe lawsuit. No more clubs."

Piecing together her lover's disjointed statements Sofia gathered he was ordered to marry her because he was told wives cannot testify against their husbands in America, although this was not entirely true in every case. There can be exceptions.

Nevertheless she realized his marriage proposal was an attempt to silence her.

After thinking about his words and not happy but eager to overlook his reasoning for his marriage proposal she swept aside her doubts, as usual. She was smart enough to realize that if she wanted to marry Karim she needed to do as he wished. She told him she'd write up a list of guests to be invited, and went to get a pen and notepad. When she returned with them Karim objected vehemently, snatching the pen from her hand.

"No family. No friends," he said, his expression irate.

"What?" she said. "No guests? Don't be silly, honey. Surely this is not the way weddings are handled in Saudi Arabia."

"No one come."

"Are you nuts?" Some of the old Sofia surfaced. "My family's coming whether you like it or not."

"No. No one. Only you and me. At courthouse. Or no wedding, Sofia."

"Why are we in such a rush? I need time to get my wedding dress made."

She knew that, as was his wont lately, he was not about to answer questions he didn't like or for which he had no credible reply. Yet, puzzled at his silence on such a significant matter but too excited to give it much thought, she found her large notepad and began sketching a simpler version of the gown she had envisioned years earlier, thinking her mother could probably run it up much quicker than the earlier, elaborate design she'd sketched as a teenager. She'd envisioned a chiffon veil and a train trimmed in Galician lace, topped by a modest bridal tiara of tear-shaped crystals.

"No, no time. We marry very soon. Civil."

So who needs a tiara, she thought. She already felt like a princess about to marry her prince. Could she let the man of her dreams slip through her fingers for the sake of insisting on a big wedding? She wrestled with her feelings for several minutes, thinking that later on they'd have the kind of wedding she had always wanted, when he didn't feel so pressured by whoever was giving him such stupid orders. Besides, as a Jehovah's Witness, although non-practicing, she knew that the religion accepted and honored civil marriage ceremonies.

"Okay, Karim. So we'll get married at the courthouse. When are we going to buy our wedding rings?"

"You go. Take money from safe."

"Come on, we'll go to Murray's, that jeweler on Morrison street, the one that designs their own hand-crafted rings and necklaces. No sense sulking, Karim. Be happy."

"No."

"What do you mean, no? You don't want your friends thinking your wife doesn't deserve a beautiful engagement ring, or that you can't afford to buy expensive matching wedding bands. What's the problem?"

"Okay. We go tomorrow."

"Wonderful!"

The next morning Sofia took extra care with her makeup and hair before dressing in the black dress that was Karim's favorite and slipping into her highest-heeled strappy black sandals. She accessorized her outfit with a silver pendant and chain he'd given her for her birthday. Today was the culmination of her wishes for a wonderful life with a wonderful man despite his occasional outbursts and going out without her. She was aware that the lives of Middles Eastern wives were different to American wives but figured she could, little by little, subtly change him once they were married.

Karim parked on the street outside Murray's. Before she got out of the car he asked,

"You have money, yes?"

"No, you should to use your credit card for this, not cash."

Karim took his wallet from his jacket pocket, removed a Visa card and gave it to her, remaining in the car.

"Aren't you coming in?"

"No."

"But they have to measure your finger."

She waited while he got out and they went inside together. The salesman brought out several trays of engagement and wedding rings and jotted down their finger sizes. Sofia took her time studying the sparking jewels the salesman laid before her. She picked out four rings she liked, two of them combined engagement and wedding rings, and asked Karim's opinion. He told her to make her own choice, which she did, trying on a gold band mounted with a pink diamond and rubies on each side.

"Now it's your turn, Karim. Which wedding ring do you like?"

Barely looking at the trays of men's rings the salesman brought out Karim pointed to a plain, narrow band.

"This one."

"That's a good choice, sir," the salesman said. "The band is 24-karat gold. Would you like both wedding bands inscribed? No? Understood. We'll have all three of the rings ready in two days," the salesman promised after Karim paid with the credit card. "We will call you."

Sofia left the jewelry store walking on air. Despite Karim's grumpy attitude she was thrilled that she was actually going to marry him.

Chapter 27

The hastily-arranged wedding took place four days later on a dismal morning on January 16 at the Multnomah County Courthouse in downtown Portland. The historical, starkly-designed centuries-old building was hardly the beautiful setting Sofia dreamed of for the occasion but she told herself it was the marriage ceremony that counted, not the venue.

On the way Karim drove past a McDonald's, "the scene of the crime," Sofia reflected, then corrected her thought to "the scene of the most wonderful connection of my life." With a typical teenager's ability to switch quickly from one viewpoint of a matter to its opposite, she determined not to let anything spoil her day.

Karim paid an extra $5 to waive the three-day waiting period when he and Sofia went to the clerk's office to fill out the marriage license application. His signature was a small Arabic glyph above the typed-in-English version of his name. He listed his age as 23 years and his occupation as "Student" from the U.A.E., not, as Sofia remarked later, from Saudi Arabia. She signed her full name, added her age as 18, and listed herself as "Homemaker." Both of their addresses were declared on the form as Lake Oswego.

Only the Circuit Court judge and two clerks were witness to the marriage between Sofia Wainwright and Karim ibn Riyad. It was a brief ceremony. Sofia was too excited to notice that Karim still had a sour look on his face. She wore an off-white suit Karim bought for her a month earlier, before the rape episode. On her head was a white, pill-box hat of the style made popular by First Lady Jacqueline Kennedy. Around Sofia's neck was the single strand of pearls that Karim gave her a few days after he was arrested. Although he didn't give her a wedding gift Sofia tried to make the event as traditional as possible by asking Anne to loan her some money to go shopping and buy her fiancé a pair of cufflinks for the French-style shirts he sometimes wore. The cufflinks Anne found and sent to her sister were fake gold but looked real.

Sofia's outfit was a far cry from the glamorous ivory satin wedding gown with a long train she had sketched for her mother to make from the time she was a fourth grader. Instead of a tiara, the hat she wore to the courthouse was perky and she fixed it in place with hatpins atop a hairstyle of smooth waves.

Maybe her wedding night would be special. She talked herself into believing that Karim had planned a surprise. Surely when they arrived back at Lake Oswego there'd be a reception at the clubhouse. Her mother would certainly be there, and Anne, of course, waiting to welcome the newlyweds with champagne and a wedding cake. Sofia knew it had all been a last-minute rush but Karim loved her and would want this day to mean as much to him as it did to her. Surely he was planning something to mark the occasion.

Alas, none of the bride's expectations came true. As soon as Karin arrived home from the courthouse, all the while refusing to respond to his new wife's animated chatter, he dropped her off at the apartment and drove away. Perhaps, thought Sofia clinging to hope, he's gone to pick the guests up and wants to make sure that everything at the clubhouse was ready for the reception.

After two hours Sofia took off her wedding outfit and dressed in jeans and a sweatshirt. She sat in one of the large recliner armchairs Karim had rented and wept until she felt no more tears could possibly flow. What had gone wrong?

The doorbell rang. When she answered it four Arabs came into the hallway.

"Karim?"

"He's not here," she said, embarrassed by her red eyes.

The visitors shrugged and continued on into the living room. They sat down and began talking to each other then moved out to the patio where she was sitting reading a magazine, The men sat on the wicker sofa. Sometimes they laughed and looked at her furtively. Finally, irritated, she stood up and approached them.

"Look," she said, holding her left hand in front of their faces and waving it back and forth. "Karim and I are married. See, this is my wedding ring."

The men shrugged. "No understand."

"Oh yes you do. I know you do. Well, that's all right, pretend all you want but the truth is here on my finger."

After an hour the men left, and two hours later Karim came home. Sofia greeted him expectantly but he made a series of phone calls and ignored her, then told her to get changed.

"Oh, I knew you were planning something. Shall I put my wedding dress back on?"

"Sure, it is nice dress."

"Where are we going?"

"Jaipur House."

Sofia hurried into the bedroom to fix her hair and change into the off-white suit she'd worn to the courthouse. I bet he's arranged some kind of reception there, she thought. However, they were shown to Karim's usual table. No one occupied it and Sofia's heart sank once again. Why couldn't he at least have invited Anne and her boyfriend to be with us?

The next day the relatives that Karim said would be living with them arrived and numbered three, not two as she'd been told. The younger men whom she took to be students were accompanied by an older man. None of them greeted or talked to her and appeared surprised to find her there. The students held a conversation with Karim and, with the knowledge of their language, she realized they were talking about her. Karim shook his head a couple of times as if disagreeing with them, which gave her comfort.

The Middle Easterners took possession of the two guest bedrooms after Sofia showed them the linen closet for towels and where glasses and supplies were kept in the kitchen cabinets. She assumed they came from upper class families as the brand of their luggage was, like Karim's, Gucci. They wore well-made suits, shirts and ties, and their shoes looked brand new.

After a week one of the students left. The remaining student and the older man held daily talks with Karim and joined the other visitors when they sat around the coffee table and continued to study the photos they had taken weeks earlier. Obeying Karim's order not to interrupt their talks she hugged to herself the knowledge that surely she would soon be on more equal terms with the Arab community as Karim's wife. It would all be different then.

Sofia debated whether to call her mother. Too ashamed to do so, regretting she hadn't told her about the wedding days ago, she laid down on the waterbed and wondered how life would be going forward. As it turned out, nothing changed. Karim's attitude was the same as ever and they lived as they had prior to the marriage. The gatherings continued almost daily but the clubbing was curtailed. An occasional dining-out gave her a chance to wear her designer clothes and shoes.

In November of that same year her husband announced he was making another trip to the United Arab Emirates and Saudi Arabia.

"Can I come too, now that I am your wife?"

"No, of course not."

"But I'd like to meet your parents, and your brothers and sisters."

"Impossible."

After his departure Sofia called Anne and arranged lunch with her, taking the bus to the downtown diner Anne suggested. As soon as her sister appeared Sofia waved her left hand to display her wedding ring. After Anne's shock wore off and it was explained that the wedding had been a quickie, the sisters, out of touch for almost a year, began sharing childhood memories, talking and laughing over various incidents.

"That Goth period of yours was awful," said Anne. "I thought Mom would have a fit."

"She did, kind of, but she knew I'd take no notice. Thankfully, I got tired of all that black clothing and makeup." She laughed. "It took almost a whole bottle of nail polish remover to get my nails back to normal."

"How's it going with Karim? Bring me up to date."

"Oh, fine. He's off on a trip to the Middle East but let's not talk about him right now. Tell me what you've been doing."

"Sofia, I know you well enough to know when you're trying to avoid an issue. Give me the truth, what's going on?"

"Nothing, really nothing."

Sofia turned her head and called the waiter for more coffee, holding up her cup.

Anne sighed. "Okay. Aside from your marriage, of course, that you are not willing to talk about, what have I been up to? Nothing much, I'm getting bored with the job."

"Anything you'd rather be doing?"

"No, not really, I'd sure like a change of scenery. I might move to Vancouver. I have friends there."

Sofia said nothing but hoped Anne would stay in Portland. Even if she didn't see her it was reassuring to know she was nearby. After lunch they promised to keep in touch but, at Anne's shrug as if to say, I'll believe it when I see it, Sofia threw her a kiss. They hugged, said goodbye, and went their separate ways.

Karim returned to Portland ten days later accompanied by two Arabs whom he introduced to Sofia as a brother and a cousin.

"More relatives? Where are they going to stay?"

"With us for now," he said.

"There isn't much room, there's only one bed available."

With two extra guests Sofia made the best of it but there was little for her do around the house to keep her occupied. Karim made the beds, did the laundry, and prepared the meals. He even took over cleaning the house. She resorted to sketching evening gowns and other clothing but her heart wasn't in it. She was bored. Her daydreams turned into thoughts about Karim's travel. Was the trip just to visit with his parents?

Over the next two days the daily student meetings seemed to be more secretive even though there was much more laughter than usual. There were furtive looks at her to see, she surmised, if she understood what they were saying.

"Of course, I didn't have much of a clue except I recognized the words New York and bin Laden. I wondered what was going on."

Three days later she and New York City received an answer.

Chapter 28

A few minutes after 12 noon on February 26, 1993, two months after the sudden move to Lake Oswego, Sofia was alone in the living room watching her favorite soap operas. Karim and five others were sitting outside on the patio talking. Suddenly, "The Young and the Restless" show was interrupted by a thirty-second news flash before returning to its regular programming. Sofia switched the channel to CNN.

The World Trade Center's multi-story basement in New York City had just been bombed with explosives inside a stolen rental truck that was driven into the building's underground garage. Six people died and more than a thousand were injured in the blast that blew a hole and travelled up seven floors of the building. The epicenter of the attack was the underground parking garage.

The FBI had been tracking fundamentalists in New York City for several months. During the subsequent investigation of the basement bombing they found in the debris the vehicle plate of a van that had been rented the day before. When the Islamist visited the rental company and asked them to return his deposit he was arrested. Four more men were arrested and all were sent to prison for life.

According to official reports the bomb plot was hatched months earlier when two of the main conspirators arrived in the United States on a flight from Pakistan. One of their Swedish passports was quickly determined to be a fake by airport customs officials. The man was detained by agents and his luggage confiscated. Inside, agents found manuals on how to make bombs, and a bundle of anti-American leaflets

The two men were traveling on tourist visas. They immediately requested political asylum as fugitives from the forces of President Saddam Hussein and the Gulf War. One of them was released on his own cognizance and allowed into the country.

Convicted as the actual perpetrator of the bombing and receiving a sentence of 240 years was a Palestinian, Mohammed Salameh, an illegal alien who had overstayed his tourist visa by several years since arriving in 1988, the year of al Qaeda's founding.

"Victoria, doesn't this all point to how easy it was, and perhaps still is, for terrorists to infiltrate our country?" Sofia said while I checked the tape at our fifth recording session. I had no answer, and she continued telling me about her day of the garage bombing.

Rushing out to the patio she told her husband to come inside to watch the news of the bombing. All six men rushed in and sat in silence as reporters covered the event. When they saw the extent of the damage most of the men smiled. Three of them cheered. Sofia looked at Karim in horror.

"Why are they celebrating? It was a terrible thing to happen."

"They are cheering for the people who were saved," said Karim, smirking.

Sofia knew he was being sarcastic but let it pass. He was her husband now and they were beginning a new life. His brothers and cousins were still frequent visitors and guests at the house. His college friends would continue to meet but they began to show her slightly more respect although when they bowed to her she suspected it was a mocking gesture. Nevertheless, she thought, now I am Karim's wife and that surely counts for something.

Within days several Middle Eastern al Qaeda zealots responsible for the basement bombing were identified by the FBI. The suspects were reportedly led by Ramzi Yousef who was easily admitted into the United States a year earlier. He claimed and was given political asylum but immediately after the bombing he fled to Pakistan. The plot was a terrorist one, said the FBI.

The thought went through Sofia's mind, once again, how the FBI had not believed her and her mother when they reported the suspicious activities, probably terrorist plots, taking place in her home but again, she let it go. Americans were assured by President Bill Clinton, the Congress, and law enforcement agencies that the bombing was an isolated incident No one envisioned it was a buildup to an even greater terrorist event eight years later that took more than a decade to plan and coordinate, and probably longer.

Sofia learned later that Yousef and his uncle, Khalid Sheik Mohammed, also plotted to blow up a Manila Airlines plane but were thwarted. She wondered if the sheik was one of those she met at Karim's house on Front Street.

It was almost July when Karim packed his largest suitcase and told Sofia he was flying to Saudi Arabia once again for a few days. Since their wedding the relationship between the couple had deteriorated drastically. Sofia was given to understand she was now "property" that Karim can treat as he chooses. They had fierce arguments and later she wondered why she hadn't simply left her new husband and gone back into the arms of her family, either to her mother in Dundee, or taken refuge with Anne.

Karim returned to Portland once more with two new people he introduced as his brothers, Hassan, a pudgy, bearded young man who never stopped smiling, and Nafir, a more serious Arab in need of dental work on his two chipped front teeth. Like Hassan, he was bearded but his attitude was more aloof, and he barely spoke.

Sofia was told that the new arrivals would live with them along with his other brother and the cousin, making a total of six people living in the new apartment..

"I was used to a large family," she told me. "Remember, my mother had several children so Karim's relatives coming to live with us was no big deal for me. In fact, I welcomed them. They were young and we had a lot of fun dancing at home. I put on some great music and we'd just have a ball."

Erika was more determined than ever to keep a close watch on Sofia and made plans to visit once more as soon as convenient. As it turned out, almost three month later a friend of Erika's invited her to spend a long weekend with her in Portland, giving Erika another opportunity to check on Sofia without having to stay with her and Karim. This time she left Jeff in her husband's care.

The afternoon of the day Erika drove to her daughter' apartment she stared at Karim in shock. She knew he had recently returned from his trip to Saudi Arabia and when he walked through the front door and into the living room where Sofia and her mother were sitting, Erika's mouth fell open. No longer the clean-shaven, well-groomed Arab she met earlier, he now wore his hair to his collar and slicked straight back with grease. He had grown a small, trimmed beard, and it was obvious he'd had surgery on his nose. A small but prominent scar on the back of his left hand, that he told Sofia he'd had since childhood, had been removed. His dark eyes were the most startling. They were encircled with black kohl eyeliner. The effect, to Erika, was strange and disturbing.

She noted that Sofia appeared to accept this new look. As the visit progressed, Erika was troubled to see that her daughter was more and more under Karim's thumb yet seemed fine with it. Why had her high-spirited and strong young daughter changed so much, she wondered. She would soon learn the answer.

On the second evening of Erika's visit, Karim took them to a Lebanese restaurant, leaving the python in its fish tank. Seeking time alone with her daughter, she told her during the meal that she would take her shopping the following day. Karim immediately objected. Sofia said nothing. The shopping trip didn't materialize. Instead, they stayed home and Karim ordered pizza for delivery.

The following day he cooked a vast amount of food for lunch which surprised Erika until ten friends arrived to eat with them. The large group appeared nervous, fidgety, and Erika wondered what was going on. Again they all smoked and drank liquor which she knew was contrary to their religion.

Karim, for the first time, tried to make her mother feel at home and took them both to Sofia's beauty salon and paid for the services while he went to a nearby barbershop.

"You see how generous he is, Mom. I come to this salon twice a month, and we both get regular facials and massages."

Still a teenager, decided Erika. I sure hope she matures soon.

Feeling uncomfortable at the tension that was frequently apparent between her daughter and Karim, Erika left to go back her friend's house. She told Sofia she'd come back and take her out to lunch her the next day. Again, the offer was shelved because Sofia said she and Karim had plans and he had told her they'd probably be out until nightfall. She said that she'd call her mother in Dundee at the weekend.

Erika took the hint but her fears increased. While Karim was not physically violent towards his wife his constant, hostile criticism and fault-finding, especially in front of others, was painful to witness. Erika couldn't fathom his reasons except that he seemed these days to be irritated by everything American. If he and his friends don't like it here, she asked Sofia, why don't they go back to their own countries? Erika wished she had the courage to ask Karim that question but knew it would cause more trouble for her daughter.

Erika's trip back to Dundee took longer than usual as she drove more slowly, worried about the questions swirling through her mind. She knew that Sofia didn't take kindly to advice from her mother, she never had growing up, but that rebellious nature had all but disappeared. What could Erika do to open Sofia's eyes to her situation? Surrounded as she was by foreigners who disdained her and estranged from Anne, Erika still had no answer when she arrived back home in Dundee.

A week later Karim's other brother and cousin came to stay with them and they all began to make frequent trips down the southern coast to La Jolla, taking Sofia along to a large Spanish-colonial mansion on a couple of acres that stretched behind an Olympic-sized swimming pool and two hot tubs.

The upscale, artsy town boasted some of the most beautiful coastal areas on the Pacific Ocean. Surrounded by bluffs and caves, La Jolla was home to celebrities such as author Raymond Chandler who set his last Philip Marlowe detective book, "Playback," in the town. Famous for La Jolla landmarks including the Torrey Pines Golf Club and the La Jolla Playhouse, it struck Sofia as a curious choice for Arabs to settle in, if only temporarily, given the fact that a giant concrete Easter cross and war memorial commanded a view over the entire town from Mount Soledad.

Sofia was told that a sheik lived in the mansion but she never met him. During their visits they were often joined by several other young Arabs. The first time they arrived at the estate, for that's what it appeared to be to her, one of the four garage doors was open and Sofia saw that it housed a red Ferrari.

Soon a handful of visitors whom she'd never met before drove up in high-end sports cars. In the house Sofia and Karim were greeted by an older Arab whom, she was told, was helping them all with some of their schoolwork as well as advice about American customs and culture. Again, the only "schoolwork" they studied in the dining room were maps, photos of buildings and landmarks, diagrams of airplanes, and what appeared to be official documents. Six cameras, large lenses, and various parts of other camera equipment were laid out on top of a low oak cabinet.

One time, when she couldn't resist her curiosity, she arose from her chair to look at the materials. She was quickly and rudely shoved aside and forbidden to see what was spread over the dining table. Karim took her arm gently and led her back to her chair.

"Sofia, stay here, please," He appeared embarrassed by her behavior. "We have to do this work."

"What's with the pictures of those planes?"

"We take flying lessons in San Diego."

"Why?"

"Many Americans have own planes. Wouldn't you like it, too, some day?"

"Wow, Karim, that'd be wonderful. But from those diagrams it looks like the planes are huge, like commercial airliners. They have tons of seats."

"No, no. You mistake it. We will learn first on flying small plane. Now please, it is better you go into the TV room."

"What do you mean by 'first?'" That implies you are going to learn to be a pilot for an airline. I'm not stupid, you know. What's going on?"

"Come," he said taking her arm in a firm grip

He led her into a cavernous room with a massive television mounted on the wall at one end faced by five rows of comfortable green recliner armchairs. He fiddled with the TV's remote control device, showed her how to use it, found a movie channel and left her alone, the first time for two hours. During subsequent visits he left her for longer periods of time. She didn't mind at first, it was their way, she knew, and at least Karim brought her along with him. But as the number of visits increased she grew more and more irritated. Sitting by herself her mood also turned introspective. Karim did not appear as happy and carefree any more, she thought.

"He often looked stressed and took his emotions out on me," Sofia said to me, "because he knows I see it in his face. He treats me with less respect, too and he didn't stand up for me when his friends made hand gestures to me to indicate the door. He became much more serious. Why did I allow him to tell me what to do and when, and order me around without explanation? His friends, whoever they are, seemed more and more suspicious of me. I wondered if there were changes ahead."

Perhaps his loyalty to her was shifting, she reflected. When had he switched from loving husband to cunning manipulator? It must have been so subtle and even innocuous that, in her teenage embrace of all things Karim, she didn't notice the gradual, insidious way he began to denigrate her, her family, and America.

Now, at 18 years old, Sofia discovered she was married to a man she was beginning to believe had a secret agenda, with brothers who might or might not be brothers, and who made more and more frequent trips to Saudi Arabia and the U.A.E.

What could that agenda be?

Chapter 29

Erika's next visit to Sofia was again without Jeff. Still anxious about her daughter's welfare she found her stay did nothing to curb her apprehension. In fact, it increased. On the first evening Karim said he had to meet some students at their home. As soon as he left Sofia took her mother into her bedroom and lifted out a black leather attaché case from Karim's closet. It was embossed with a symbol she assumed was his family crest.

"I'm going to break into this case," she said. "I'm sure he's cheating on me. I bet he has photos of other women in here."

Taking a couple of different screwdrivers from a kitchen drawer Sofia attacked the lock. After a few attempts it sprang open and she pushed back the lid.

"Good heavens," said Erika. "Look at all those passports. There must be seven or eight of them."

She picked two up and flipped them open. She looked at the others. Three were British, one German, one Swedish, another Israeli, and the other two passports were American They all bore Karim's head shot but each gave him a different name. The attaché case also held several official-looking documents in Arabic. Four of the documents had Karim's photo, and had green borders.

"Sofia, this is scary. Put everything back. It's not women's photos he's hiding in here, it is fake identities with aliases."

"Mom, he's a foreigner, maybe he needs lots of passports when he visits different countries."

"Oh, Sofia, that's the most ridiculous thing you have ever said. Where's your head at? I wish you weren't so naïve. He's using fake identities. Why are you so trusting of this man? You used to be so smart. Use your brain as to why these documents are here. Look at these magazine covers, too. What's this all about and why do you think he keeps them?"

Sofia took two of the magazines from the case. They were glossy publications with red borders, similar to Time magazine. She gasped as she studied the photos. Although taken from different angles, both covers showed a large group of Arabs in traditional dress sitting around a circular dining table. She pointed to two of the men.

"That's Karim's father, Bathshar, and his brother Zafir. I saw a photo of them both with the family once. Look, here's Karim's father on another magazine. I don't know who the others are or why their photos are there."

Erika kept silent. She told me later that she instantly recognized the dictator president of Iraq,

Saddam Hussein. Who was Karim's father to be in such exalted company?

"Can you close the lock so he won't know?" said Erika.

Sofia arranged the contents as closely as she could to the order they were originally in and pulled down the lid. The lock clicked closed easily and only showed a couple of faint scratches. She tucked the case back into the closet. In the living room Erika was agitated.

"Please pack up your things and leave with me right now, Sofia. We'll go back to Dundee. You have no idea who this man is or what he's doing. I don't trust him. He's obviously hiding something. Please, dear, do as I say. I am begging you."

"No way, mom. I am staying. I don't understand what all those things in the case are either but I love him. I am sure there's an explanation. We love each other. He'd never do anything weird to hurt me."

She told her mother that Karim trusted her so much he used to allow her to handle his banking.

"When I came to live here he took me to his bank and showed me the bank statements. There were large deposits and withdrawals. He really trusts me, Mom. I handled a lot of his bank stuff. I put in large sums of money, dollars as well as dirhams, that's the currency they use in Saudi Arabia, and whatever he tells me to bring back here I put in the safe. He gave me the combination numbers.

Sometimes I help him wire money off to his friends. Isn't he a wonderful guy?"

Erika left the next morning to drive back to Dundee knowing her stubborn daughter would do as she pleased. As soon as she arrived home Erika called Alan, ten years older than Sofia, asking him to call his sister and give her some serious advice.

"Mom, she'll do exactly as she wants," Alan said. "She's always been that way. Let's just hope she comes to her senses soon. Tell you what, I have another business trip to Portland for the insurance company coming up soon. I'll stop by and say hello."

Fraught with fear that Karim might take Sofia to Saudi Arabia forever, or take her there and then abandon her, Erika told me that she spent more and more time with her daughter, spacing the visits a few months apart.

"I visited four or five times, Victoria. I knew I still couldn't say a word against him but I wanted to reassure my youngest daughter that I cared about her and that her family would always welcome her back."

Chapter 30

Shaken awake before dawn on a rainy day in May, 1993 Sofia was surprised to hear Karim tell her to start packing.

"Why? Are we going somewhere?"

She still harbored hopes of a trip to her husband's home country in the Middle East. She envisioned a palace with fountains in the forecourt and formal gardens; sumptuous gold-trimmed sofas and chairs, and exotic furnishings throughout. There'd be pools with white water lilies and stone sculptures shaded by hanging plants.

"We move to San Diego. You will like."

"What? San Diego? Why are we leaving Portland? I love Lake Oswego."

"I change college. I register already at San Diego City College. Look," Karim said, taking out his wallet, "My new student visa. I get yesterday from Saudi Arabia embassy in Washington."

The card he flashed quickly at Sofia and returned to his wallet was similar to a driver's license complete with photo ID. Her description of it reminded me that there was a recent report in the Los Angeles Times of a major student visa fraud case that involved a California forger. He created hundreds of fake visas for foreign students, mostly for Arabs from Lebanon, Saudi Arabia, Kuwait, the United Arab Emirates, Turkey, and Qatar. The newspaper article also reported that the U.S. Immigration service said the suspected forger was so inundated with fake visa requests he hired a staff and even took the students' exams for them for a large fee.

"But, Karim, you have only been here two years and student visas are valid for five. Then they can be extended, that's what Stefan told me. Besides, you hardly ever go to school any more. Stefan said students are deported if they don't attend school full-time."

Karim looked at her sharply. "Why are you questioning me? Get luggage. Pack. Come on!"

A quick learner under Sofia's tutelage Karim was mastering English at breakneck speed. She'd picked up a several words of Arabic but nowhere near the conversational ease and self-assurance with which Karim now expressed himself in her country.

Satisfied and relieved he was taking her with him to San Diego despite the coldness that was growing between them Sofia began taking her clothes from the closet and dresser and folding them into the Gucci suitcases.

"Are we taking everything, and will the moving company bring it all to San Diego?"

"No," he said. "We take nothing. Only clothes. Rashad will live here."

"Another one of your cousins? You have so many I can barely keep up with all the names. Who else?"

Karim ignored her question and told her to hurry up. They would travel by car, he said. He had recently leased the latest Mercedes-Benz sedan, the $122,000 S-Class. After driving Buicks he moved up to Lincoln Town cars and Cadillacs. Finally he moved on to German models. The cars were always black four-door sedans. Sofia was interested to see which of the latest cars he'd bring home as he changed them so frequently. She figured he enjoyed showing off in them. Often, he insisted his friends take a walk-around of the car, pointing out its advanced features.

"I was surprised he never leased sports cars," Sofia told me. "When we went to the Mercedes showroom he always stopped first to look at the convertibles. Then he'd tell the salesman he needed a large model because he had many friends visiting from abroad. I felt like adding, yes, hundreds of brothers and cousins but, of course, I kept my mouth shut."

Excited at the prospect of an adventure, of moving to a new city, Sofia told herself perhaps the change would mean an improvement in their relationship. Since returning from his latest visit to the

Middle East her husband was extremely distant towards her. Gone was the loving and caring he previously showed. Instead, he ordered her around like a servant. What happened to him while he was away, she wondered. Has he fallen in love with someone else? Someone back home? She found out later that while he was in Saudi Arabia he married the woman he'd been betrothed to at birth. It didn't bother her too much, it was their custom, she told herself. Karim was here and the other woman wasn't.

If he was tired of her Sofia figured he wouldn't want to take her with him to San Diego. Reassured, she did his bidding and gathered her belongings. She knew he would pack his own clothes as he'd never liked her touching his things.

Before the couple left she called McDonald's to leave a message for her sister. Although they had been mostly estranged over the past year she told the cashier she was going on a trip and would call Anne again later. She was still annoyed with Karim for not allowing her to celebrate her 18th birthday with her sister. Instead he took her to Jaipur House for dinner, and gave her a gold bracelet.

By 7 a.m. the car was filled with luggage, the bong pipe, and the prayer rug. Karim emptied the contents of the safe into a metal case and wrapped and boxed his coffee pot and cups. The trunk of the car was already half-full with large leather suitcases she'd never seen before. The python was to be left in its aquarium, he said. Told they were ready to leave Sofia took one last look around the apartment and went out to the car. Instead of waiting for her husband to open the door to the passenger's front seat she opened it herself and went to get in as usual.

"No. Sit in back, Sofia."

She looked up to see Karim getting into the driver's seat and his brother Haroun walking to the passenger door.

"Is Haroun coming with us?"

"Yes."

There was little conversation along the way. When the cousins talked it was in their own language and they never addressed her. Sofia was happy enough to watch the scenery speeding by and dreaming a few dreams but in the back of her mind were questions: would Haroun be living with them? What kind of housing had Karim found? When was he there to house-hunt? She didn't remember him ever telling her about a trip to San Diego before the one they were taking now.

They stopped twice along the way at gas stations and convenience stores. She found out from the manager at the first 7-11 store that he estimated the trip driving from Portland to San Diego would take about 17 hours to cover the 1,000 or so miles. A long day, she thought, and it means we'll get there close to midnight and I won't be able to see much.

As it turned out her calculations were slightly off because as they approached northern San Diego, near San Clemente, an imposing sight dominated the skyline not far from the Interstate 5 as it ran close to the Pacific Ocean. Rounding a large bend in the freeway no driver could miss the massive twin domes of the San Onofre nuclear plant soaring 200 feet into the air. Set between two beaches, the nuclear reactors faced the waves treasured by surfers but were off-limits since the plant was built. The distinctive domes were protected from the ocean by a tall seawall and from the public with stern warning signs noting it was private property and trespassing would result in rapid prosecution.

"Look!" said Haroun, pointing to the domes. "Generating station. Nuclear. We take pictures," speaking in English and showing off his command of the language.

"No, they close down, my brother. One dome already shutting," said Karim, explaining that the plant was built in 1965 and provided electricity to surrounding areas. "Last year the first dome, Unit 1, was decommissioned," he added, lingering over the long word. "Other dome also soon. Many protests here. Thousands of people. Environmentalists."

Sofia nodded, not commenting. The fact that Haroun wanted to take photos of the plant made her feel uncomfortable although she didn't know why, she was later to tell me. Perhaps he regarded it as a tourist attraction. She watched Haroun approach the perimeter fence with his camera. Large signs posted at regular intervals along the fence were painted in black letters reading: NO WARNING. NO WARNING SHOTS FIRED.

Resuming their trip, the sun already down and night approaching, Haroun read out the written directions to a suburban community in the northeastern sector of San Diego. A sign announced it as Rancho Penesquitos with several estate-sized Spanish-style houses. Sofia perked up. She liked the fact it was a gated community and the homes were large. Karim parked in the driveway of the house indicated by his brother.

Leaving the luggage in the car they went inside. The house was furnished luxuriously. Heavy dark blue velvet drapes hung at the floor-to-ceiling windows that looked out onto lush landscaping, and the white oak flooring was covered in places by Persian area rugs.

"This is beautiful," said Sofia, inspecting the living room, dining room, office, and kitchen. A wrought-iron balustrade curved up the stairs to a second floor. She ran up to find five bedrooms and four bathrooms plus three walk-in closets.

When she came downstairs she saw that the suitcases had been brought in but hers were not among them. Maybe she had to bring them in herself. A new Karim rule? She knew Haroun would certainly not touch them because they belonged to a woman but Karim used to be more courteous.

Ignoring the slight she asked Karim why such a large house was needed, although she was already in love with it.

"Which bedroom is ours?"

"No," he said. "I have apartment for you not far away."

"An apartment for me? What do you mean? We won't be living together?"

"No. Many cousins and uncles are soon coming here. You remember Rhamzi Atta? He will come, and Uncle Abdullah."

Speechless, she followed his order to get back in the car. Again, Haroun sat in the front seat reading out directions. The first-floor apartment they stopped at proved to be in the same neighborhood as the house and four streets away. Karim and Sofia carried her luggage inside after Karim gave her the key to the front door. The interior décor was beautiful but she was still puzzled at this strange turn of events. If he doesn't want me with him then why did he bring me to San Diego, she wondered. What other arrangements is he making? Consumed with jealousy, suspecting an affair, Sofia felt completely lost and abandoned.

"I still loved him with all my heart," Sofia said to me later. "He was my one and only. Looking back I know I was stupid to put up with his behavior towards me but I was so in love nothing mattered except being his wife. I guess he played on my vulnerability. I had no self-esteem, no confidence left. I sobbed myself to sleep, unsure of anything anymore."

Chapter 31

At 9 a.m. the next day Karim arrived at her apartment to take her grocery shopping. He appeared remorseful and explained that he was forced to live apart from her because of his uncle's orders.

"Maybe he will change. I'll talk to him when I go home again."

"Another visit to Saudi Arabia? You just got back from there."

He shrugged. "Come, get jacket. We go to supermarket."

After they returned and he filled his wife's apartment fridge with food Karim quickly said goodbye. He told her he was on his way to the airport and would come to visit when he returned. He left with just a kiss on her cheek. She was so absorbed at her plight that she forgot to ask him how she was to get around before he drove away. She realized she was unable to go anywhere without a car. She wanted to explore the community and find shopping other than grocery stores. Then she remembered she had no money. Whenever they went out Karim paid for everything. At least she had a telephone.

Depressed and lonely, Sofia called Anne, crying on the phone as she told her of the situation she was now in. Her sister was outraged at the news, that Sofia had been taken to San Diego, set up in separate living quarters, and then been left with no car and no cash.

"Don't worry, sis. I want to quit this job at McDonald's anyway. I told you I was bored with it. I'll start driving down early tomorrow and I'll be there before you know it."

Reconciled with Anne, Sofia's mood lifted and their reunion was jubilant. Anne settled in and for the first three days they drove around the city and beach areas in Anne's car to explore their new environment. Both knew they needed to find jobs and Anne was instantly successful at an upscale restaurant. Sofia was hired as a front office receptionist at a plastic surgeon's clinic, not surprisingly because of her beauty and youth. She was still only 19 years old but, she joked to me during our recording sessions, that at times she felt closer to fifty.

After he returned from abroad Karim began stopping over to her apartment to take her on trips with him to Mexico. But, as she was to find out, they were not for pleasure nor because he wanted to be with her. Anne was not included, Karim said, because there was no room in the car.

"No room? This car is huge, it can seat seven people. What are you talking about?"

"No. We meet friends in Tijuana and bring to America."

"I was surprised but happy to go with him," she told me. "I guess he was using me and maybe it was the reason he brought me with him to live in San Diego. Or perhaps this was the beginning of our relationship getting back on track. In Mexico we went to nightclubs in Tijuana with names like The Red Mustang and Very Best Rock and Roll. They were cave-like places, dark and low-ceilinged, like underground caverns. I loved Mexican music, it was so happy and upbeat. The people at the next tables often translated the lyrics for us, saying they were praising the success of the drug cartels and the murders they committed. I thought the songs were bizarre but Karim said they were funny."

At both clubs they met up with people Karim said were his relatives or friends and they'd end up coming back to San Diego with them in the car. This happened five or six times. Some were people who had visited Karim from Saudi Arabia when she and Karim lived in Portland. On the drive back Karim always told her to keep her fair hair uncovered when they went through the border crossing so the guards could see she was American.

"Occasionally, while driving to the clubs we were stopped and questioned by the Mexican federales with their guns drawn," she said. "They'd stand in the middle of the road and motion us to stop. They threatened to confiscate our car until Karim took out his wallet and paid them off."

The group of Arabs, including Karim, wore business suits under Arab robes, which they took off and left in the car before entering a club. On the return trip they would don the robes again to pass as non-Mexicans. If the border agents asked any questions about the purpose of their visit to Mexico and wanted to see their IDs Sofia was expected to supply the answers.

"We never had any trouble getting back into the U.S." she said.

After the third trip to Mexico her sister told Sofia she should go to the FBI office in San Diego and tell them what was going on with all the Arabs coming in illegally.

"Why can't they come in on student or tourist visas?" Anne said, pointing out to Sofia she could be arrested for being part of bringing in not only illegals but possibly terrorists. After a few days Sofia agreed to Anne's suggestion. She called the FBI and left a message. She never received a call back, for which she was pleased because ten days later Karim came calling once again for another trip to Tijuana. She treasured those dates.

In 2021 there would be reports of the U.S. border patrol arresting two known international terrorists from the Middle East who were trying to enter the United States illegally as part of the open border policy of the President Joe Biden administration.

One weekend, in an agreeable mood, Karim took Sofia out to lunch, then to a flying school on the outskirts of San Diego. It was a sunny, cloudless June day and the weather, the flight manager told them, was perfect for beginning the flying lessons Karim and his friends wanted to take.

In addition to small and larger private planes parked at the airfield a scattering of colorful hot air balloons occupied a huge portion far off in the distance, with launch and landing areas. The designs on the balloons' huge skins were a riot of colors, ranging from red and blue stripes, the colors of the rainbow, and Disney character faces. Off to one side two balloons were being assembled. Nearby, passengers were climbing into the wicker baskets of three other balloons ready for take-off. Four balloons were already ascending; others drifted high overhead, and a couple of balloons were still on the ground as their passengers listened to pre-flight safety briefings.

"Are we going somewhere in a plane, or taking a ride in one of these balloons?" said Sofia. "You seem so excited about something."

"I am going to learn to fly," he said, puffing out his chest in a way she'd learned to recognize when he felt a sense of pride. "We all are."

Four of Karim's friends, cameras slung around their necks, came over to them in the terminal building and they all went off to sign up for lessons in small planes, leaving Sofia alone. She didn't mind as there was so much to see. Small aircraft took off and landed; instructors walked students to board their planes for flight lessons, and the hot air balloons provided a festive sight.

She wandered around the airfield and finally went over to the vast area at the far end to admire the balloons. She talked to their pilots, laughing as they told her each passenger needed to be weighed before taking a ride in one of the terminal's rental balloons. There were several private balloons that she admired too as she inspected the baskets, some larger than others, and watched the owner of a balloon finish decorating it for a wedding celebration. A salesman was walking around handing out balloon tour brochures and she eagerly accepted one.

As it turned out, her husband was not a good candidate for flying lessons. When she returned to the terminal and found him inside he told her he had become airsick during a test flight to give him and the others a taste of what they'd be learning. The pilot was forced to cut short the flight and bring the plane back to the airfield for Karim to alight.

Sofia persuaded him instead to take a ride in a hot air balloon. He agreed after watching a few that were already airborne. He told Sofia, laughing, that their speed was perfect for him, at which she joined in his laughter. After they landed they watched the other Arabs still going through their paces in the sky. When they landed Karim told them about his ride, pointing to the balloons. The others eagerly agreed to take rides. When they were aloft they took aerial photos of the view including the Pacific coastline and the port, and farther out to sea where a U.S. aircraft carrier was anchored.

Karim never made a second trip to the flying school, telling her he would only take commercial jets and only as a passenger, a prophecy which would be fulfilled when he boarded Flight 175 on September 11, 2001.

Chapter 32

Sofia soon suffered another shock that shattered her world. In April, 1994 Karim told her he was starting divorce proceedings. The news sent her into a tailspin. Despite his treatment of her, his neglect, and the knowledge he had already married the woman in Saudi Arabia, Sofia still held out hope he would change back into the loving man he had once been during the early days in Portland.

When she expressed such hopes to Anne, her sister shook her head in disbelief, asking Sofia how she could possibly entertain such a thought, or would even want Karim back.

"I'm glad you've been married only a couple of years to that jerk. You are well rid of him," she said.

Anne by now had already moved in with her new boyfriend, Stanley, a British tech expert who was part of the so-called "brain drain" phenomenon. American companies began raiding the United Kingdom's high-tech businesses for their most skilled employees. Luring them with double their current salaries and offering low loans for homes,

186

the companies paid the passage for hundreds of engineers and scientists to cross the Atlantic to accept the offers. Stanley was hired to join a biotech lab in downtown San Diego.

Sofia was enjoying her job as a receptionist at the plastic surgeon's office. Her salary allowed her to buy clothes more appropriate for a doctor's clinic and she'd been able to save up enough money to put a deposit on a second-hand car. Her living accommodations were fine and she managed to enjoy a social life, going out with work colleagues and with her sister to a few favorite clubs. However, the impending divorce cast a pall over everything she did. She was devastated.

Over the next few days a small conviction persisted at the back of her mind that she and her husband would reconcile and live together again. She clung to the hope that he missed her.

"A week later Karim came over with a fistful of papers for me to sign," she told me. "I knew there was no sense protesting. I put my signature on whatever he directed me to. I didn't get a lawyer or even ask anyone for advice, and I didn't ask for alimony. He wouldn't have even known the word. I didn't tell my family, either, until much later although I kept Anne up to date. I was numb and just went along."

In mid-December, 1994 Sofia received a Final Judgement of Dissolution of Marriage from the Superior Court of California, County of San Diego.

The document was signed by both parties, Karim in his small, cramped Arabic characters and Sofia with her usual large artistic flair. She failed to request that her former name be restored as the Court would have allowed, but she did take back her maiden name of Wainwright at a later time. No grounds for the divorce were entered on the official form and Sofia doubted she even read the papers she signed, barely able to see them through her tears.

Life returned to routine. Sofia received an increase in salary, and had a few dates with men she met at the clubs and bars but none of them turned into a serious relationship. She found it difficult to focus on a boyfriend when her heart still yearned for Karim. She wondered where he was, what he was doing, if he'd left America and gone back to the Middle East permanently.

Seven months later Sofia couldn't resist placing a phone call to her former husband, hoping to rekindle their love. He picked up the call with an expectant Hello? Hearing her voice his tone instantly changed.

"What do you want?"

She could imagine his frown and his usual expression of annoyance when the caller wasn't the person he thought it would be.

"Karim, I am still in San Diego. I'm sure you are as miserable as I am about all this. Please don't shut me out. Tell me we can meet."

"No. Impossible."

"Why? You know I still love you. If it is impossible to meet after all we meant to each other tell me this – what was our relationship for? What was the purpose of marrying me?"

"You will never understand," he said.

He hung up without saying goodbye.

She drove by the house once, debating whether to ring the bell until she saw the For Rent sign in the driveway. So, he'd left. Where had he gone?

Chapter 33

Suspecting that Karim was no longer anywhere in San Diego, Sofia decided to leave too, and return to Oregon. There was no reason to hang around if he'd gone. She gave her notice at work, packed up her belongings, said goodbye to Anne, and drove north. Her spirits lifted the farther she drove, telling herself she was leaving behind every memory she had of Karim ibn Riyad. It was finished. She would start a new life, maybe in Portland, maybe in Dundee. Wherever she landed she was determined it would be completely different to anything she experienced over the last three years. Still a young woman, barely twenty years old, she told herself a new life lay ahead.

Sofia returned to Dundee. Her reunion with her mother was blissful and for two weeks Sofia basked in the love that surrounded her. She kept in touch with Anne who stayed in San Diego, having found a more promising job and becoming engaged to her boyfriend. The Wainwright siblings all came to visit with Sofia in Dundee, spending a day or two, but she soon became bored. The friends she had made in high school were either scattered to other states, or had married and were involved in family life. Despite her effort to forget her former husband, her past experiences and feelings of abandonment returned time and again. She needed to stop moping around in Dundee and hit the big city again, get a job, and build a career. Her beauty attracted attention wherever she went. Men often stared at her and several still asked for dates but she felt empty inside.

"I wasn't interested in having a boyfriend," she said. "I still didn't know the reason for the divorce from Karim. I suppose he was ordered to split with me, just as he'd been ordered to marry me, but it was weird. I couldn't figure it out."

Sofia decided to leave Dundee and move back to Portland. Her hometown was still too quiet and rural. Erika well knew that her daughter craved more excitement than the small town was able to offer. She'd had a taste of the bright lights and she still had her whole life ahead of her.

Erika made arrangements for Sofia to live with the same friend in Portland that Erika had stayed with when she made a visit to Karim and Sofia's Front Street apartment. It would be a temporary fix until Sofia could find a job and a place to live.

Thanks also to Erika's contacts in the fashion industry Sofia was hired at the same upscale Portland department store she had worked for as a salesgirl and later as a shopper and wife of a wealthy Arab. This time she was hired as an in-house model. With employment secure Sofia needed a place to live. The store had a bulletin board in the employee café where Sofia found an ad seeking a roommate. It was posted by one of the women working at the perfume counter. Sofia soon moved in. The apartment was small but she had her own bedroom.

She avoided the nightclubs, restaurants and bars she'd enjoyed with Karim and instead went dancing and attending rock concerts with new friends. Occasionally, during the summer, she and a friend from work, Margot Lincoln, drove three hours north to Seattle for a mid-week mini-vacation on their days off, staying with the woman's parents.

Sofia was finally succeeding in banishing all thoughts of Karim and the life they had led together but at an outdoor café in the Port of Seattle, a place she remembered well from the afternoon Karim's brother went scuba-diving, her life took another turn.

While sitting on the café patio overlooking the harbor with her friend a waiter brought over two demitasse cups of coffee and two small bowls of whipped cream, placing one in front of Sofia and one in front of Margot. The waiter explained the offering was from "the gentleman at the next table who would like you both to savor Turkish coffee."

Both girls looked over the person indicated who raised his own demitasse cup to them in salute, and smiled. A tall, dark-haired handsome man of around thirty-five years old in a T-shirt and jeans, he wore a sweater slung around his shoulders, the sleeves casually looped and tied over his chest in the manner of European men. Sofia giggled and held up her cup to return the greeting.

"May I join you?" he called over. His spoke with a Caribbean accent but Sofia couldn't place it.

With eyebrows raised in question she looked at her friend, who nodded.

"Sure," said Sofia. "Thank you for the coffee. I am familiar with it as I used to enjoy it every day in Portland."

Damn, she thought, why did I have to say that? I'm trying to forget that life and all the habits I got into.

"Ah, I will come there," said the man, transferring his cup to their table and sitting down. "It is wonderful to see such beautiful women. You light up the day. Do you live in Seattle?"

"No, we are both from Portland but we come up here sometimes on our days off. Are you visiting? Where are you from?"

"Originally from Haiti. I am half Haitian, half French. I went to live in Paris at 18 years old and begin a career there. I am the owner of several Starbucks shops in France and I come here to meet with the Big Boss but I must confess I like Turkish coffee best," he said. "Please allow me to introduce myself. I am Christian Leroy Beaulieu."

"A grand and impressive name," Sofia couldn't help remarking. "I am Sofia Wainwright and my friend is Margot Lincoln."

"Ah, like the cars."

"Yes," said Margot, "the same spelling but sadly no relation."

Christian made it obvious he was interested in Sofia but gallantly asked both of them for their phone numbers. However, it was clear which of them attracted him. When Margot said it was time to leave and drive back to Portland he asked Sofia if he could call her.

During the trip home Sofia asked her friend what she thought of Christian, and received a non-committal shrug in return, saying she bet he was married although he wore no wedding ring and probably had at least one mistress in the French tradition. Sofia agreed and they turned to other topics.

Two weeks later Christian called Sofia and the two began an affair, meeting either in Seattle or Portland. Their romance blossomed and Sofia hoped for a more permanent relationship with him, her fantasies focusing on living in France, maybe even somewhere along the French Riviera. She thought about brushing up on her French. But after three months, when he left for Europe, she never heard from him again. She suspected he was married because he walked away from her at times to take private phone calls, but she didn't have the nerve to ask him.

"Another foreigner?" said Anne when Sofia confided in her. "Why can't you find a nice American boy?"

"Look who's talking! You're engaged to a foreigner yourself."

"Yes, but he's English, almost the same as us."

The liaison with Beaulieu had a result that changed Sofia's life, forcing her to quit her job. She was pregnant. Should she have an abortion? It went against all her principles, as well as her religion which, although she no longer practiced it, was ingrained. Sofia decided to have the child. She moved back to her mother's home, spending the final two months of her pregnancy in Dundee. Sofia gave birth to a healthy, sturdy baby boy she named Cody.

The new living arrangement was a godsend at first with Erika looking after her grandson when Sofia started working at the only department store as a sales manager and model. Cody thrived in the small town atmosphere and the love of his grandparents. But again Sofia, in her early twenties, was restless.

Once a month she drove from Dundee to Portland to meet up with friends from her earlier time there, and frequented their favorite dance clubs. At one point she was asked by one nightclub owner if she'd like a job as an exotic dancer. Sofia considered the idea because the money he said she could make was extremely appealing but because she was thinking of taking up her religion again she declined the offer.

Sofia continued her social life and one Saturday night at a Portland cowboy bar a tall rangy customer wearing a plaid shirt and jeans caught her eye. His name was Preston Jarrett, a farm hand from the small town of Felicidad in Northern California. Single, young, and divorced like Sofia but with no children, he sought out some excitement on his off days and spent part of his weekends staying at a friend's Portland apartment. They joked about the fact they both had blue eyes although Jarrett's were a darker color.

The bar scene was their favorite outing and beer the drink of choice although Sofia drank less than her date. They went dancing but not as frequently as she would have liked. Neither of them were inclined to share their previous marriage experiences and Sofia was pleased to keep hers hidden. She gathered from a few of his remarks that Jarrett's marriage, the wedding held in a Las Vegas chapel, was very brief and ended well by mutual consent. She confided that she had married an Arab in Portland and that he and his friends were strange. She still didn't understand their behavior she said during the courtship with Jarrett and that she had just blown it off as foreign customs. She told him that her past was well behind her.

"Preston wasn't interested in what I told him," she said, "and I was glad he didn't want to pry into that part of my life."

Soon, Sofia and Jarrett were dating regularly and sharing a couple of joints. He denied he was an addict and only smoked on weekends. The couple were quickly an item and after a few months Jarrett proposed. Sofia, finding a man she felt would give her and Cody a decent, normal and uncomplicated life, accepted. They were married in Felicidad and this time her family attended the wedding although the event was modest and confined to close family members. Sofia designed a modified version of her dream dress and Erika added her own touch to it with pearls sprinkled on the neckline and cuffs.

Sofia's new husband, she soon learned after their marriage, was not only the weekend weed smoker he told her he was but also a small-time drug dealer and often skipped work to make better money from addicts. Because of her experiences during her time with Karim's friends who smoked marijuana she was not surprised at Jarrett's extra-curricular activities but she was determined to keep Cody away from such influences.

A year after their marriage Jarrett and Sofia welcomed a baby son, Benjie, and within eighteen months another boy they named Hank. Both blonde-haired, the boys had Jarrett's dark blue eyes and quiet disposition. Close in age, they were more like twins than older and younger brother, while Cody enjoyed being the Big Guy.

With the added expense Sofia took a job as a waitress in nearby Merced, California with Sally

Jarrett welcoming the daily babysitting of her grandsons. Sofia and her husband settled in to what was considered a normal life in Felicidad, occasionally driving north-east to Portland or down south to the Merced River for a day of fishing.

"I was so grateful to leave my past behind me, that whole horrible, sad time with Karim. In fact, I was so busy with the job and the three kids I didn't even think about him for years," she said, her fingers twisting the base of the microphone as I recorded her words onto yet another cassette tape. "Not until after September 11, 2001 when I saw his face on television and in the newspaper as one of the hijackers."

Chapter 34

As she learned more about the 9/11 attacks over the following days Sofia was shocked, like all of America, to hear and read about the lives of the hijackers. Some of the reports struck her as so off-base she reached for the phone to call the FBI to set them straight about the Arabs she knew, then thought better of it. Her family's warnings to keep quiet about Karim played again and again in her mind.

Suddenly plunged back into her past, speechless at the thunderbolt that shook her heart, mind, and soul Sofia listened to the newscasts with mounting fright. Although Karim's meetings with his friends and their many discussions had given her a feeling of disquiet, of something not quite right, she didn't believe that what she was suspecting back then was really true, that they were terrorists.

It was not until after she mentioned their activities to Erika in 1992 that Sofia had begun to take her suspicions more seriously. When she and later she and her mother went to the FBI offices in 1993 to report the strange activities and were practically booted out of the office, she decided to clean the slate, so to speak, throwing out anything that reminded her of Karim. She burned his photos in a garbage can in the tiny back yard and donated the designer clothes Karim bought her to Goodwill. She had left her marriage certificate and other documents with Erika, and told her to burn them, too. It was a request that her mother ignored, instinctively deciding they were valuable if only to her. She saved them in a metal box along with photos of Sofia as a child.

Television and print media coverage of the 9/11 events was all-consuming to a public mystified then furious and finally outraged at the audacity of the terrorist attacks on U.S. soil. Again, comparisons to Pearl Harbor were debated although the former was an act or war and the latter an act of terrorism. Pearl Harbor was in response to a known enemy, Japan, and the bombing of the U.S. warships was supported by that country's people. The 9/11 events were perpetrated by members of a terrorist group, al Qaeda, and not backed by all Muslims. The Japanese were the first to use airplanes for suicide missions, flying directly at and into their targets. Were they the inspiration for the al Qaeda suicide attacks on the World Trade Center?

According to reports, the FBI listed the names of the hijackers, which flight they were on, and the role each pilot played once they were on board and in their assigned seats. Karim, or Aswad al-Abadi, as the FBI identified him, was not one of the pilots.

"How could he be?" Sofia remarked to me. "He hated flying to the Middle East and back because of jet lag and his fear of heights. He told me he never looked out of the window after take-off. Heck, Victoria, he almost threw up his lunch in a hot air balloon!"

Nevertheless, Karim and his brother Zafir boarded Flight 175 as "muscle men" as the FBI described them, taking their seats in the first rows of cabin class. The "muscle men" phrase amused Sofia because Karim, she said, was as skinny as a stick.

"He was a puny, short guy," said Sofia, "whose only participation in sports or physical activity once in a while was bowling and billiards, hardly the kind of occasional exercise that built biceps. In fact, most of the 9/11 operatives were between 5 ft. 7 in. and 5 ft. 8 in. in height, according to the U.S. Government's 9/11 Commission Report."

In the Report's timeline the Boeing 767 took off from Boston's Logan International Airport with Karim and Zafir listed by United Airlines as Saudi Arabians and the other hijackers on the flight listed as being from the United Arab Emirates. Each of them checked baggage and took their assigned seats. The departure time was 8:14 a.m. and the final destination was Los Angeles International Airport in California. Flight 175 carried a crew of nine and fifty-six passengers, among them five listed as Middle Easterners. One of the two terrorist pilots sat in first class, the other pilot sat in business class. The three other terrorists were in the main cabin.

The twin World Trade Center towers were the tallest buildings in the world at the time of their completion. Each tower contained 110 floors. The entire complex held seven surrounding buildings, all of which were destroyed or demolished due to fires from falling debris during and after the attacks, and also to damage from the cleanup and recovery process.

Early on the morning of Thursday, September 11, 2001, perfect flying weather along the East Coast, everything appeared routine. Two of the doomed flights, 11 and 175, lifted off from Boston's Logan airport in Massachusetts on time, and Flight 77 left from Dulles in Washington D.C. Despite the fourth plane, Flight 93, taking off forty minutes late from Newark, New Jersey, all four of the airliners departed within forty-four minutes of each other. All 19 hijackers had gone through Security with no problem except for two of Karim's fellow hijackers on flight 175. These men spoke barely any English. The United Airlines agent had to speak slowly and repeat her questions about security before allowing the Arabs to proceed.

The four planes were to carry five al Qaeda hijackers on each flight. However, a later investigation revealed that one of the terrorists had been refused re-entry into the United States a month earlier because he had overstayed his visa. It was no longer valid. Thus there were nineteen hijackers instead of the planned twenty.

At 8:33 a.m. Flight 11 reached a cruising altitude of 31,000 ft. The two hijacker pilots made their move, bursting into the unlocked cockpit between 8:42 and 8:46, killing the captain and first officer. Akram al-Nassim, who had trained as a pilot in Florida, took over the controls and Tamir ben Farran sat in the co-pilot's seat after dragging the bodies of the two United Airlines pilots out the door. Although no details were able to be provided later the bodies were probably thrown into the aisle of the first class cabin.

The other terrorists on board also made their move, threatening passengers and the flight attendants with knives and Mace, and stating there was a bomb on board. As soon as it became clear what was happening a stewardess ran to the back of the plane and grabbed a phone to make a report of the hijacking to air traffic control. These details were from accounts of the people that the passengers and crew called and who were able to relate what was happening on board.

The first plane to reach its assigned airspace following ground control's instructions was American Airlines Flight 11 carrying eighty-one passengers and eleven crew. The pilot was cleared to climb to 35,000 feet. But there was no affirmative response from the cockpit to indicate that he had either received the message or was preparing to obey it. Communication appeared to have failed. After several attempts to reach the airliner, which by now had clicked off its transponder, a supervisor was told of the situation. Alarmed at the plane's silence, the controller contacted American Airlines, which also failed to establish communication with its plane. Suddenly, a transmission was heard from Flight 11 instructing everyone on board not to make a move and included the statement, "We have some planes." At this point it was clear the airliner had been hijacked. At 8:46 a.m. the hijacker pilot of Flight 11 aimed the plane directly into the upper floors of the World Trade Center's North Tower.

United Airlines Flight 93 was forty-two minutes late taking off from Newark because it was held up on the crowded runways. It was a popular time of the morning to fly to its destination, San Francisco airport, scheduled to arrive, as usual, before noon that same day because of the three-hour time difference. There were 37 passengers and a handful of crew on board. At 9:28 a.m. a communication from ground control was acknowledged by the pilot. The next sounds heard by the controller were a series of shouts. The plane descended to 700 feet. Then he heard, "We have a bomb on board." News of this additional hijacking was quickly passed up the chain of command. It was determined that the plane was northeast of Camp David, the U.S. president's country retreat in Maryland. Several passengers and crew heroically stormed the cockpit at which point the pilot sent the airliner into a steep dive, crashing nose-first into a field in Shanksville, Somerset County in rural Pennsylvania. All on board died.

Flight 175 carried sixty-five passengers, seven flight attendants, and two pilots. Three of the passengers were children under the age of five years old, twelve were women, and the remaining thirty-five were men. Just after take-off, at 8:14 a.m., one of the other planes, Flight 11, was being hijacked. The crew on Flight 175 reported they overheard what they described as "a suspicious transmission from another plane," which later was determined to be Flight 11.

Inside Flight 175's target, the South Tower of the World Trade Center, the daily working life of those in the offices and, in one case, a kindergarten, began as usual. Twenty of the higher floors in the South Tower were completely occupied by Morgan Stanley employees. At first everyone in the South Tower was unaware that a commercial airliner had crashed into the North Tower but the terrifying noise of the explosion nearby caused many to leave the building, encouraged by the in-house fire warden. Hearing the directive, the entire personnel at the Morgan Stanley offices were then told to evacuate immediately.

It was the policy of all airlines to train their personnel to be non-confrontational in the event of a hijacking. Some of the passengers used the United

Airlines' phones positioned in the backs of some of the seats to call and attempt to reach their families and friends to tell them about the take-over by terrorists, and describing how some of the passengers and crew had been injured when the al Qaeda Arabs threatened them with the Mace and knives.

By 8:51 a.m. Flight 175 had drastically changed altitude and direction and, flying erratically, turned towards New York. This caused the plane to have two near mid-air collisions, the first with Delta Airlines 2315 flying from Hartford, Connecticut to Tampa, Florida, and moments later with Midwest Express Flight 7 on its way from Milwaukee to New York. Both planes were frantically directed to take evasive action away from Flight 175, which they did.

At 9:02 a.m. the airliner with Karim aboard sliced head-on into the South Tower of the World Trade Center like a torpedo, between floors 77 and 85, its progress watched in disbelief, horror and shock by television viewers all around the world. At 9:59 a.m. the building collapsed, seventeen minutes after Flight 11 had crashed into the North Tower.

Chapter 35

"I've sometimes wondered," Sofia said to me, "how Karim felt as the plane headed for its target. Did he throw up? Was he one of the last to board to delay his fear? What was he thinking when he buckled himself in? He knew it was a suicide mission. They all knew. He must have been aware he was going to die. Karim had barely lived his life but was not only willing to give it up, he was part of a mission that would kill thousands of innocent people. I can't imagine what mind training can plant and feed that kind of an obsession."

It wasn't difficult to understand. I thought of the many cults and pseudo-religions that thrived in America and around the world, including the Branch Davidians, the Manson Family, Heaven's Gate, the People's Temple, and many others. Most of them led to tragic endings of innocent, obsessed, or misguided members. But al Qaeda was no cult. It was far worse. A multi-national terrorist organization founded in 1988 by Osama bin Laden, it was composed of a network of radical militant Sunni

Islamists dedicated to killing those they considered infidels. Who did they call an infidel needing to be killed? Anyone who was a "disbeliever."

The horror wasn't ended with the destruction of both iconic towers at the World Trade Center. A third commercial plane, American Airlines Flight 77 bound from Washington, D.C. to Los Angeles, was hijacked forty-one minutes after take-off with fifty-eight passengers and four crew aboard. It was among fourteen other planes that ground control at Dulles airport was handling in its sector and all seemed well. Not until thirty-three minutes later did the plane deviate from its flight plan, turned south towards New York, and disappeared from ground control's radar screen. A U.S. Air Force Search and Rescue team was requested to look for a downed plane after reports of a huge spiral of smoke but searchers looked to the west instead of east, where the hijacker pilot had turned the plane. Closing in on Washington, D.C., Flight 77 was said to be six miles from the White House. At 9:37 a.m. the hijackers pointed the plane towards the Pentagon in Arlington, Virginia and dove down, striking the southwest wall of the Pentagon.

The attacks were the second on American soil, after the bombing of Pearl Harbor in World War II. The U.S. military, the president, Congress, and law enforcement all over the country scrambled for answers. In Felicity, Sofia was equally in shock. Her husband had already left for work when the hijackings occurred, and Sally was at the park with the three boys, so both were unaware of the tragedy.

It was only when she arrived back on her street, at noon, adjacent to the shopping area, did Sally realize something terrible must have happened. Not a single car sat in the usually-filled spaces along the street nor in the parking lots. Every store was shuttered. She hurried home with the boys, saw the newsreels, and called Sofia.

Chapter 36

Sally knew nothing of Sofia's first marriage. Her son, Preston, had shown no interest when his new wife told him she'd been married before, although not to Cody's father. As her mother-in-law never mentioned it or inquired about her first marriage, Sofia assumed her time with Karim would stay buried.

After 9/11, when she saw his photo, that expectation crumbled.

She'd had three years of peace with Jarrett, was blessed with the two boys, and had come to terms with her Preston's quirky lifestyle. He was always affable, she thought, probably because of the weed he smoked, and thankfully he hadn't moved on to other drugs. She'd seen only too well while clubbing how destructive were cocaine, heroin, and especially opium that some of Karim's friends used.

"It's not fair," she complained to Erika on the phone "I've put all that old stuff behind me. Will I never be free? Why can't I just live in peace?"

"You can, honey, if you just stay quiet. You've got a beautiful family now. Say nothing I'm sewing a pair of matching overalls for the boys."

"Mom, how can you think of stuff like that right now?"

"Takes my mind off the dreadful horror of it all, Sofia."

At the Angus Grill, days after 9/11, Sofia became so distracted over her dilemma she was threatened with being fired after mixing up orders and forgetting to give customers their bill. Adding to her indecision about contacting the FBI was hearing constantly about the attacks. They were, understandably all anyone talked about as Sofia went about her waitressing. There was no escaping the words "Twin Towers," "terrorists," "al Qaeda," "Arabs," and 'hijackers."

Every radio and television station, every newspaper and magazine was overtaken by the need to answer the how-and-why questions. There were no early official explanations. Not until much later did details emerge as to the handling of the four events. Where were America's fighter planes, touted as the most advanced ion the world? Why was security so lax? How about any intelligence ignored over the past several months and even longer? It was recognized that al Qaeda must have been planning their attacks for a long, long time. It was reasonable to assume that while America basked in its reputation as the most powerful nation in the world, the U.S. government was supremely confident no one would dare attack.

The terrorists' coordination of the four commercial flights, within an hour of each other, pointed to a master plan and probably much rehearsing. Did the hijackers fly on those airlines several times earlier, taking those specific flights, as if they were conducting a military drill? They called themselves Soldiers of God and martyrs to their cause.

Sofia searched her soul for an answer to her question including how many red flags she must have missed. Confiding her fears to Erika, she was reminded that they had twice warned the FBI. But her mother's words were no comfort or solace.

For five days after the revelation that Karim was on Flight 175 Sofia continued to agonize over whether to talk to the FBI. Would she put her family in danger? What would be the consequences for herself and her children? Every hour, it seemed, whether she was at work or at home, she went back and forth debating if she should reveal she was married to one of the hijackers, or try once more to forget her past life with him. But she knew in her heart what her decision would be. She confided her fears to Jarrett but he appeared disbelieving of her story and asked no questions. When Sally called Sofia to commiserate over the attacks on innocent people Sofia, who had always kept her past hidden, shared her grief and quickly hung up the phone. She needed more time to consider what to do.

On the sixth day of mourning the almost 3,000 people who died including children she knew she'd regret it forever if she kept her secret. Sofia thought she might have information she didn't realize she possessed. Perhaps there were telltale signs she dismissed that the FBI would think were significant, and could jog her memory for details. She remembered when she and Erika shared their frustrations back in the 1990s when they went to the FBI in Portland and San Diego and were treated with derision.

"These aren't female fantasies, sir," Sofia remembered her mother telling the FBI agents. "These are real activities we have both observed that appear to be a conspiracy, or at least preparing for an attack by terrorists."

Another thought struck Sofia. What if al Qaeda came after her? And what will everyone think of her, married to a hijacker? How will she handle the shame? What about her son in school, and the two babies? Now 27 years old, she's sure no one will believe how she could have been so naïve years earlier. She could barely believe it herself. What a fool she'd been. Her recriminations, I discovered during our interviewing sessions, were a constant self-flagellation. I had no words of comfort to offer that were different to Erika's. Sofia's decision to talk to the FBI had to be her own.

Eventually, integrity blended with guilt won out. Sofia knew she couldn't live with herself if she failed to act, knowing she possessed what could be crucial information for additional attacks. Her family was still urging her to stay silent, calling every day except for one brother, Alan, whose words resonated with her. As it turned out his advice and her decision to follow it was the start of her second living nightmare and was to become her legacy.

Now light years more mature than when she was a runaway Sofia sought out the government's hotline phone number that had been set up and called the Sacramento office of the FBI.

Chapter 37

"What is the reason for your call?" said the female voice on the other end of the line. Her tone sounded peremptory and strained.

"I have some information about a few of the hijackers," Sofia said.

She'd been almost surprised when someone finally picked up. She had tried the number several times before slamming the receiver into its cradle in frustration when no one answered, even after letting it ring 20 or more times. But she kept her temper. She could imagine the frantic activity going on in every FBI bureau around the country, in every CIA office around the world, at Interpol, and from continent to continent. Few knew it but the Diplomatic Department of Security that provided protection to U.S. embassies and consulates around the world also joined the hunt.

The FBI and other U.S. agencies deployed thousands of agents after the 9/11 attacks and urged citizens to come forward if they had any tips, pointers, or knowledge that pertained to 9/11, to the hijackers, or to terrorism. One imagines the floodgates being opened with such a plea but it was mostly writers – journalists and authors – who slid back the bolt to unlock the answers to al Qaeda's war on America.

During her call to the FBI Sofia was asked to repeat her earlier statement and was told to hold while she was transferred. After several minutes doing so she debated hanging up the phone but then a man's voice came on the line and identified himself as a Special Agent. She told him that she was once married to one of the 9/11 hijackers and that they were divorced several years ago. When she described their activities with cameras, the flying lessons, and that some of the terrorists were guests at her house, she was asked for her address and told a Special Agent would visit her.

The morning following the phone in her bedroom rang at 6 a.m. Half-asleep next to her husband, Sofia ignored it. Who'd be calling so early on a Sunday morning? She picked up the receiver then dropped it back into the cradle, annoyed that the loud ringing would wake the children. The phone rang again three minutes later. As before she lifted the receiver and dropped it back down. The third time she picked up and answered, thinking belatedly it could be an emergency, someone from the family, perhaps.

"Hello?"

"Mrs. Jarrett, FBI agents from our International Terrorism Unit will be arriving at your house in fifteen minutes."

So, she thought, she was finally being taken seriously. Prescott turned over lazily and asked who it was. Sofia didn't answer. She jumped out of bed and went to the side window. A black Chevrolet Silverado pickup truck was parked opposite the trailer. Two men exited, stood around talking, and occasionally glanced at her door. She quickly washed her face and dressed in jeans and a shirt. She asked Prescott to tell Cody to get up, and have Hank and Benjie dressed and ready to go out for breakfast while she had her meeting with the agents.

Her husband's nonchalant response to what was happening struck her as a little odd but not really surprising. She reminded herself that he never showed much emotion to anything these days unless he was out of weed and needed money for a hit. He wandered around half awake, it seemed. If their kitchen jelly jar contained even a few coins from tips she made at the Angus Grill he'd empty them into his pockets.

A few minutes later Jarrett walked out of the second bedroom with the children and nodded to the agents without saying a word. He checked his wallet, seemed satisfied he had enough cash for their meal, and left with the three boys. Sofia breathed a sigh of relief. She didn't want her husband or Cody to hear her rehash details about her previous marriage. Not that Jarrett would care much, she reflected. Sofia glanced in the bathroom mirror, saw how pale her face was, and brushed pink blusher onto her cheeks. She had mixed emotions about this visit, not sure

217

whether to feel nervous or thankful that what she knew of her hijacker husband and his so-called friends would hit a receptive ear. A firm knock on the front door brought her to open it. The men she'd seen from the window earlier were standing at the top of the four steps that led up onto the small front porch.

"When I opened the door to the FBI agents," she related, "they looked like they were straight out of Central Casting. They fit the mold of everyone's idea of an FBI guy so perfectly. Both were well-built, one more bulky than the other, wearing dark suits, red and black striped ties, and white shirts. They had buzz-cut hairstyles and carried black briefcases."

After picking up the kids' toys from the floor, stashing them in a cardboard box in the bedroom, and closing the door she invited the agents to sit at the built-in dining table with its red plastic padded bench seats. Before sitting they both opened their briefcases and laid out notebooks, pens, and two large identical tape recorders. Sofia sat opposite them.

The two men quickly introduced themselves, offering their business cards that identified them as Special Agent Henry Walker and Special Agent John Falucci. The cards bore the seal of the U.S. Department of Justice Federal Bureau of Investigation, with a scales of justice illustration and the motto underneath, "Fidelity, Bravery, Integrity," book-ended with sheaves of laurel leaves. Thirteen stars represented the thirteen founding states. The cards included the agents' names and division along with their field office addresses.

"Can I see your badges, too?" she asked, remembering the fake documents Karim hid in his attaché case.

Walker and Falucci reached inside their jacket pockets and placed their metal badges on the table. They showed a distinctly different and simpler design to the business card, with large FBI initials embossed in the center and surmounted with an eagle. Sofia picked the badges up, fingered them, and handed them back to the agents.

At first the agents were polite and well-mannered, Walker took the lead in asking questions while the other handled the recorders. Both wrote notes. But as Sofia told them more and more of her story and about her relationship with Karim ibn Riyad, as she said she knew him, they started looking at her with suspicion and disdain, the same way Karim's friends used to look at her when they visited Karim's Front Street and Lake Oswego apartments back in Portland.

Walker pressed his lips together and frowned while Falucci tried to appear expressionless but his mouth was turned down in obvious disapproval. The more she talked the more grim the men's faces looked as Sofia revealed detail after detail of names, meetings, activities, and locations. She told them of the people she heard mentioned or had met including Atta, Sheik Benihammad, Yousef, and Khalid as well as frequent mentions of al Qaeda and bin Laden. The agents wrote the names down as the tension in the room escalated and within an hour she saw their derision and disbelief fully expressed. The questions thrown at her grew more mocking and again and again her answers appeared to be disbelieved.

"You claim you went to the FBI field office in Portland and San Diego. There is no record of such visits."

"That's not my fault. Maybe your agent there didn't think our warnings were worth making a note of. But I assure you, I made the visit, and so did my mother. I also went to the FBI in Portland back in 1993."

It became more and more obvious to Sofia that she was making a terrible mistake by notifying the FBI of her previous marriage to Karim, the 13th hijacker.

Chapter 38

"Were you really married to him?" The question was asked with a jeering smirk. "Muslims don't marry American girls so what kind of a tale are you telling us?"

Sofia brought out the marriage license and divorce decree, pointing out Karim's Arabic signature and its English translation printed underneath. She told them about the several passports and papers she'd found with different names attached to his head shot. She showed them the only photo she had kept of him where he was sitting in the booth with the French fries at McDonald's in Portland. She described how the Arabs loved fast food, and how they behaved at the nightclubs, their talks around the coffee table covered in maps and photos, and her recognition of the name Osama bin Laden.

"Who did you meet from your husband's family?"

"Only two who Karim said were brothers, and some cousins. I never met his parents but his father used to talk to me on the phone after he finished speaking to Karim. Here's his number in Saudi Arabia."

The agents asked about her family. As it turned out, they already knew the names of her parents and siblings, where she went to school, how she experimented with meth in high school, and that she was a Jehovah's Witness. They'd obviously done their homework before coming to see her.

"Now I was really scared," she told me. "I just sat there trembling while they took lots of notes and tape recorded everything. Their questions were short but pointed and were asked sternly like a schoolteacher with a student. My guilty feeling got worse as they questioned me, their demand for details came so fast. I must have stuttered because they often told me to repeat what I had just said."

Where did you meet your hijacker?

How did you meet?

Tell us about each date, where you went.

Tell us everything you know about his parents.

What were the exact dates that your husband flew back to Saudi Arabia?

How often?

Describe the friends.

Give us their names.

Tell us where they took photos.

Describe the maps and blueprints.

Where did they go to college in Portland?

What did they study?

Describe the apartments in Portland and
  San Diego.

Where did they take flying lessons?

What kind of aircraft?

What did you talk about?

Tell us about the house in La Jolla.

How were these men financed?

Who was the money man you met?

Which banks did they use?

Why did they trust you?

She launched into a detailed account with names she knew, which make and color of car each one was told to buy or lease, and where they lived as far as she remembered. She had only gone to two of their residences in Portland and hadn't taken note of the addresses.

"Did they use any words like bombs, detonators, timers, or explosives?"

"I don't speak Arabic, as I told you, sir, so I don't know, nor did I recognize anything close to those words. These guys were focused, as far as I could see, on selecting targets. Aside from the planning sessions Karim was also in charge of recruiting, I think."

When she told the agents that the Arabs were split up into groups they appeared much more interested, looking at each other significantly and asking for details. She enumerated the seven teams the men were divided into and explained the role of each team as she understood it.

"Group 1 were noisy and arrogant," she said as the tape recorders whirred. "They were provided with computers, money, and upscale cars. Group 2 were quieter, rarely frequented the clubs. They were the photographers, and took trips with us to Seattle and other areas. Group 3 were stand-offish, one of whom was a 17-year old. This group occasionally dated American girls. Another lived at what I was told was a safe house."

Group 4 were errand boys, given very little money and no cars. They apparently worshipped Karim and hung on his every word. Two of them lived at Lewis and Clark in dorms. The fifth group appeared more educated than teams 2 and 3. Sofia got the impression they weren't seriously into al Qaeda but liked to hang out with bin Laden's supporters. One of them had a long braid down his back and never, in her presence, expressed anti-Americanism, unlike the others. The 6th team, whose four members were the first of Karim's friends she met, were all from the U.A.E. and grew up together, attending the same schools.

The largest team was Group 7. Most of them had moved to Portland from Seattle. They drove red, yellow and silver sedans, never black. They were engineers, navigators, and skilled professionals, she was told by Karim, who said she should respect them even though they were rude to her. While several of the other members invited Karim and Sofia to their homes for parties and gatherings Group 7 stayed aloof from personal hospitality. They often called Karim on the phone to ask for meeting dates and times. If Sofia answered the phone she said they called her one of the many English curse words they had learned.

"They called me a bitch and a few more choice words in Arabic that I recognized. I always responded with a laugh," she said. "I was often called a 'kafir,' meaning 'infidel,' or 'non-Muslim' and in a sarcastic tone I was sometimes called, 'habibi,' meaning 'beloved.' I didn't let any of the names bother me."

Sofia explained to the Special Agents how she took checks Karim received from abroad to the bank and brought back envelopes of cash. She said that with her help he opened bank accounts with $3,000 and $5,000 initial deposits using documents issued by the embassies and consulates of Saudi Arabia and the U.A.E. The accounts were all at small branch banks of larger banks. Withdrawals were made using bank debit cards validated for two or more names. Addresses that were given to the banks and accepted were post office box numbers.

She denied any knowledge of savings accounts or safe deposit boxes being rented. There were several times when the Arabs failed to understand overdrafts and exceeded the cash limit when the cards were used. Karim whose name was always added to each account, was constantly calling to find out the balances in the various accounts. Deposits and disbursements followed no consistent timing or dates, and none were attributed to paying normal living expenses for rent, utilities, car payments, or insurance, Sofia said.

The myriad list of questions seemed to have no ending as she was constantly asked to provide more details although she was convinced they already knew everything about her, Karim and his friends. Sofia told the agents how the Arabs she knew, except for Karim, never talked with Americans unless they were hookers or pole dancers; how her sister Anne was eventually banned by Karim from visiting Sofia in Portland, and how Karim changed his appearance after a visit to Saudi Arabia.

"I was asked how come I was allowed to be there at the meetings, to see, to listen, and even occasionally voice an opinion without being told to go into another room, as was always the case when we visited the La Jolla house," Sofia said. "I told Walker and Falucci that Karim insisted I was to be treated with respect. But when we moved to San Diego it all changed."

Sofia said that Karim's general attitude was a contradictory puzzle to her. He would laugh at American holidays; he considered American mental abilities far inferior to Middle Easterners; claimed that their countries were much safer; and that the U.S. justice system was flawed. On the other hand he loved the freedom he enjoyed in the U.S. and the lifestyle.

"He never expressed hatred for America or Americans like his friends always did," she said. "I often jumped in to their conversation when I knew what they were discussing, such as when they made ugly faces if the name of President Bill Clinton or baseball came up."

Judging by the materials the Arabs studied she told the agents she believed that while 9/11 occurred on the East Coast, the cell members she observed with their photos and maps were plotting for the West Coast to be hit next, and that the terrorists were not as interested in landmarks as much as generating large body counts.

"They wanted to kill thousands of people at a time, with one big blow at their targets. That was their intent. They weren't as interested in destroying significant individual landmarks as much as how many people were inside," she said. "Did their study of architecture help them plan exactly where to point their planes at the Twin Towers? Was the collapse of the buildings factored in?"

Sofia was given no answers and finally, after three hours, the agents packed up their equipment and took their leave, warning her to say nothing about their talk. She assumed that her answers to their questions was the last she'd see of them. She'd told them everything she could remember of her relationship with Karim. At times their probing brought back details she had forgotten but quickly remembered as she cast her mind back.

The dozens of journal pages that she filled after Walker and Falucci left became interspersed with swear words and doodles as she enumerated the questions and wrote down how she had answered, her memory now sharp and accurate. As she wrote about the intense interrogation and her answers that were challenged harshly at times during the interview she re-lived the three hours and felt nauseous. Sofia began to have heart palpitations. She started hyperventilating and was afraid she was suffering from an anxiety attack. She gulped down a handful of Valium, a sedative medication.

When Jarrett returned with the children he found his wife passed out on the floor. He picked her up and took her to the truck, sat Cody, Hank, and Benjie next to her and rushed to the hospital. The doctors and nurses, hearing her ranting about 9/11, thought she was delirious or mentally ill and asked Jarrett if he would agree to send her for a psychiatric evaluation.

Jarrett, alarmed by their diagnosis, drove back to the trailer to look for the agents' business cards she had shown him after they left. He found them on the dining table, both cards torn in half. He called Walker's number and begged the Special Agent to assure the doctors that his wife was not mentally ill because of the claims she was making.

Agent Walker, concerned that Sofia might reveal information the FBI was anxious to conceal, arrived at the hospital within an hour. He confirmed to the medical personnel that Sofia's statements about 9/11 were not delusional but merely exaggerations to questions he had asked her earlier. He impressed on the medical personnel how important it was for strict confidentiality.

Sofia was discharged from the hospital the following day. Walker called to ask if they could come back to meet with her again. Sofia reluctantly acquiesced after asking Sally, her mother-in-law, if she would take the three kids for a few hours as Prescott would be away all day. Sally arrived and took the children back to her house, telling Sofia she'd drop Cody off at school on the way as he wouldn't be riding the school bus. She promised to pick him up after class if necessary. A kindly woman in her mid-sixties with a languid manner of speaking as if nothing could faze her, she doted on her grandchildren and was always offering to babysit.

Sofia tidied up the trailer and finished just in time before the knock on the door she dreaded. Would this second debriefing physically and mentally upset her as much as the first one? To her surprise, they greeted her with wide smiles and relaxed demeanors. They brought blown-up photos of the hijackers and others they told her were possibly terrorists and again asked if she recognized any of them. They spread the photos out on the dining table, covering it completely, and asked Sofia to identify any of the men she was able to remember. She was shown the larger-than-life-sized image of Karim.

"We measured the folds of his ears," Walker said. "Ears are scientifically known to be as individual as fingerprints. Does this look like his high forehead? What about the other facial features?"

Sofia was asked again about his family in Saudi Arabia, what she knew about their residence in the United Araba Emirates, and about her former father-in-law's advisor whom Karim had told her was named Abdullah.

"We know that he is one of Osama bin Laden's many brothers," said Falucci. "There's also another Abdullah, named Mohdar Abdullah, who you might have met in San Diego?"

She replied she had no knowledge of such a man, that there seemed to be lots of Arabs with the name of Abdullah or Mohammad, and she'd paid little attention to who they were or why they were in America. They couldn't all be Karim's uncles, surely, she told herself at the time, but it didn't matter to her. She accepted that they were a brother, a cousin, or an uncle.

When I spoke to her myself later she gave me the same information, namely that she didn't know who Mohdar was. I looked the name up in "The 9/11 Commission Report" where he was identified as a Yemeni student living in San Diego. He was accused of helping two of the hijackers apply for driver licenses and other documents. Further research sent me to a German web site that stated after being arrested in late September 2001 as a 9/11 accomplice and serving several months in an American prison with no charges filed, Mohdar was deported to his own country.

It was interesting to discover that the Commission and the FBI came to different conclusions as to Mohdar Abdullah's involvement in the attacks, with continuing debates over how the hijackers managed to train as pilots of large airliners, conduct surveillance, and accomplish their murderous missions all, it seemed, without officials raising any suspicions except from a civilian who was an airfield manager in Florida and regarded the Arab pilot trainees suspicious. The two agencies came to opposing final decisions with the Commission Report claiming that Abdullah assisted the terrorists in San Diego and the FBI denying it.

As Sofia read the Commission Report I gave her on my next tip to Dundee she was skeptical of parts of it. Published in 2004, a few months before I met Sofia for the first time, the lengthy book stated that the intelligence community had struggled throughout the 1990s to find out about international terrorism. But what about the domestic terrorism that she and Erika attempted to tell the authorities about? Why hadn't she been taken seriously in 1993? It was a question she and her mother asked themselves many, many times after 9/11 and never received an answer much less an apology. She was handing them one of the 9/11 hijackers on a platter back then although she didn't know it. Why didn't the Commission Report include this failure to act in its investigation? Why hadn't the San Diego and Portland FBI ever filed a report on the Sofia's visits? One of the key findings of the Commission was that America's leaders failed to understand the gravity of the threat from Osama bin Laden and al Qaeda.

As the FBI agents continued to run several other names by Sofia, some of whom she confirmed as knowing, she was also asked to describe her ex-husband's personality. She made the agents laugh when she said that during his first week in America he believed it was such a violent country he walked around with his briefcase double-chained to his wrist and waist although there was nothing of value in the briefcase. She also managed to keep them entertained with her stories of what she used to shrug off as cultural customs including Karim's habit of laundering the sheets every day, observing his friends walking hand in hand, and having to tell her mother to leave some food on her plate as per custom during her visits.

Karim, Sofia said, was always bragging and was extremely arrogant. He often criticized America saying that the Middle East was safer, cleaner, and the criminals more severely punished. He claimed his people were more educated, while laughing at the reasons for America's annual holidays. Yet, one Christmas he decorated their apartment with a Christmas tree and gave Sofia gifts.

"Karim never said he hated America or Americans," she told the agents, "but like his friends he expressed disdain for our religions. He'd attack our women's rights and other issues."

At one point during her second meeting with the lead agent, Henry Walker, he became aggressive and she felt he believed she was lying, saying she was contradicting herself. She reminded him she was married to the man eight years ago but that most of her memories of the period were firm in her mind.

"I blocked them out until now," she told the agents, "but they were always there somewhere. I can even tell you the names of the fragrances he used. I know which brand of cologne he bought, and even his toothpaste that was imported because it was fluoride-free." She laughed. "He never went to the dentist, though, probably too scared they'd put him under and learn his secrets."

"How about doctor or hospital visits?"

"No, never. He didn't trust anyone like that. Besides, he was always pretty healthy, like the rest of them. Maybe he had check-ups when he went to Saudi Arabia."

Walker told her that the last they knew of her former husband was when he moved to New York in May, 2001, and that he and his brother often exchanged identities. Sofia told them about the passports and official-looking forms and documents that she and her mother found in Karim's attaché case. She realized, as she told the agents, that the red flags finally began to click into place like tumblers in a padlock after Erika told her no one needed different passports. Was she right to have had suspicions although hers were prompted by jealousy about other women and not a plan to murder almost 3,000 people?

As the meeting went on Sofia became agitated by the full implications of what she was unknowingly involved in back in the 1990s. She feared the agents thought she was complicit in 9/11 or at least was part of or knew about its planning. After her visitors left she resorted to taking methamphetamines, trying to erase the FBI, Karim, and everything he stood for from her mind. Exhausted, Sofia asked Jarrett take the children out for ice cream while she went to bed early. Unable to sleep, the agents' questions and thoughts pounding her mind, doubts crept into her thoughts as she tossed and turned and finally gulped down four sleeping pills.

As she drifted off to sleep she wondered if this was to be the pattern of her life from now on. If so, how would she cope?

Chapter 39

The next meeting with the FBI two days later was held at a McDonald's, a location Sofia considered ironic although it was not in Portland but Stockton where what turned out to be another nightmare began, that of working with the FBI that was to stretch into months. She arrived slightly high on meth taken to relieve her anxiety and help her overcome the hostility she felt from the agents. She was coherent and able to give the feds more exact details of Karim and the other Arabs' activities. Subsequent debriefings and interrogations then shifted from outside locations to Walker's Fresno office and included a female agent, Cynthia Lloyd.

As Sofia revealed more details she realized she possessed far more pieces to fit the puzzle than either the FBI or she herself at first comprehended. She watched the agents record her statements on their two large recording machines as well as writing down everything she told them on large yellow legal-sized notepads. Anxious not to miss a word, they listened in silence when she answered their questions which grew more and more personal, pointed, and at times offensive.

"They wanted to know about lovemaking, our daily habits, which tables and booths we sat at in the restaurants and the movie houses and what food we ordered. What could that possibly matter?" Sofia said. "And where did we buy our clothes, which barber shops and beauty salons did we frequent. How did Karim pay the bills, they wanted to know, who mailed them. Their insistence for all that stuff was nuts."

She was asked to describe in minute detail everything she could remember about the Arabs she met in her house and elsewhere, how they were dressed down to their shoes, any jewelry, especially rings, and if they had any individual or odd facial features. Did they carry firearms? Stupid question, she thought. They'd be hidden wouldn't they? It's easy to hide small guns, she told the agents. Detectives and criminals do it all the time, including you, she said.

Others members of the Wainwright family came in for additional scrutiny by federal agents. Anne was contacted and questioned in San Diego. Erika came home from grocery shopping one day to find a business card tucked under her door and two messages on her answering machine. The caller gave her name as FBI Agent Diana Salisman from Eugene, Oregon. She asked permission to pay Erika a visit, which Erika granted with a phone call.

When the agent arrived Erika found her to be a pleasant, middle-aged woman with mousy brown hair and hazel-colored eyes. She looked tired, with bags under her eyes and barely able to smile when she shook hands. Erika could imagine how much pressure the country's law enforcement agencies were under to find out every detail about 9/11.

Salisman treated Erika with cautious respect and told her that Karim was definitely identified by the authorities including the Bureau as hijacker Number 13 on Flight 175. After Erika made them both coffee and they sat at the dining table with Salisman's recording machine operating the agent asked for every remembered word she exchanged with Karim and his friends during her visits to see her daughter at their home in Portland and Lake Oswego. The agent wanted to know how he and his friends treated Sofia, if there were particular situations or events that struck her as strange. The interview was extensive and at the end of it, when the woman left, Erika felt drained.

"Now I knew first-hand how Sofia felt. It was as if the agent had wrung every single moment and thought from the time I entered Karim's apartment until we left." she told me. "I told her how Sofia and I went to the FBI offices to report possible terrorist sleeper cell activities but we were laughed at. I hope I was helpful to Salisman but it was a while ago and my memory isn't as sharp as it used to be."

Two days later, however, the agent called Erika to retract her ID of Karim and to deny she had confirmed his identity during their in-person meeting at Erika's house. Salisman claimed the ID was a mistake and told Erika to forget her words confirming his participation in 9/11 and to say nothing to anyone.

"Why she did that I have no idea but perhaps she thought I'd be blabbing all over the place," Erika told me. "But that's not my style. I am a very private person about anything to do with the family. So, if it wasn't Karim, or Abadi or whatever the FBI called him, why was Sofia still being questioned? Where is he if he's not dead under the ruins of the South Tower? Has the media ever asked questions about what was done with the hijackers' remains or tested their DNA?"

Erika decided to do her own research into her daughter's former husband's family and discovered that the name al Abadi was as common a name in the Middle East as Smith or Jones are in the West. She didn't remember many of the names of the countries she saw on Karim's passports when Sofia bust open his attaché case but she does remember the name of al Abadi on two of the passports and on one of the a documents. She concluded they were all fake.

In addition to interviewing Sofia's family the Bureau agents also visited the Angus Grill to talk to her co-workers, the manager, and the owner of the restaurant. Some of them were new hires, including the woman who replaced Sofia at the restaurant, and had never met her. The manager remembered Sofia receiving a phone call at the cashier's stand, then saying she had an emergency and had to go home. She returned to work for a few days but then phoned the manager to tell her that she was sorry but she had to quit the job.

"Who was the person who called her with the emergency?"

"I have no idea," the manager said, "It was a male but he didn't give me a name."

"How long did they talk?"

"Not long. Just a few minutes. When Sofia came to tell me she needed to leave her face was white. I asked what was wrong and if there was anything I could do but she just got her jacket and left."

"Did you meet her husband, Preston Jarrett, or see him here?"

"No. After she left her job here we never heard from her again."

The other employees were questioned briefly and had nothing to contribute except to say they heard that Sofia was a hard worker, an excellent waitress, made good tips, and was well-liked by the customers for her cheerful personality.

Special Agents at the FBI field office in Portland interviewed the Human Resources manager at the department store where Sofia applied to for a job.

"I only met her once, when she came in with her resume," the agents were told "It was so long ago I barely remember. I do remember, though, that I was impressed with her and asked her to come back a second time to meet some of our executives. With her looks and her obvious smarts I thought she could have a good career here. But she didn't call again."

Next on the FBI agents' list were the management companies that handled the Front Street and Lake Oswego apartments that Karim rented. The assistant managers responsible for the properties were shown photos not only of the 19 hijackers but also of other Arabs that were suspected of being terrorists. While each manager said they knew Karim as the tenant, there had never been any serious trouble or refusal to pay rent. His deposits were in order and at the end of the lease when he said he was moving to San Diego his deposit in the form of a check was returned to him.

"You said 'serious trouble.' What do you mean?"

"Once or twice," said one assistant, "we had complaints of late-night parties but as soon as one of our security guards went over there to ask them to keep the noise down they complied right away."

The McDonald's where Sofia met Karim was the next place to be visited. There had been a complete turnover of the staff. None were working there back in the early 1990s. Nevertheless, they were shown the hijackers' photos along with some other suspects.

"Sure, a few Arab students from the local colleges used to come in," said the cashier, "but none since 9/11. I don't recognize anyone in these pictures, these guys look older than the students who come here."

The agents visited the nightclubs, restaurants, shops, and video stores that Sofia told them about but came up empty. The Arabs were polite, quiet, and spent a lot of money, was the same answer from each venue except occasionally when they called out to the strippers.

Sofia's meetings with the FBI continued. One morning they gave her a thick black Magic Marker pen and told her to keep it with her at all times. Suspicious, she took it apart and found the tip of the pen contained a bug that she figured was a recording device. She threw it away. A replacement pen appeared on the passenger seat of her car. When she asked Walker about it he told her it was a means of communicating with him.

"Just talk into it," he instructed, "if you need to."

"What need would I have?"

"You might remember something while you're driving around that you need to tell us."

As she often did, Sofia called Anne in San Diego to give her the latest update on her activities with the FBI. Three days later Anne called to tell Sofia she, too, had found a strange pen in her car. The sisters agreed that the FBI was keeping tabs on them both by tapping their phones, and the agent didn't seem concerned if they knew it. Sofia switched cars with her husband, leaving the pen in the Honda while she drove Jarrett's pickup. It made no difference. Another pen appeared on the driver's seat of the truck.

By now she felt as if she is living in a bad movie and that there were electronic bugs all over the trailer. She complained about them to her brother Alan who told her that the new Patriot Act gave the FBI wide authority after 9/11. She also learned when she watched his press conference on C-Span that the former Deputy Attorney-General, George Terwillinger, admitted there were terrorist cells existing in the U.S. as far back as the 1980s.

"Just as I told the FBI when I, then with my Mom, went to their offices in Portland in the 1990s and said we suspected sleeper cells," Sofia said. I wondered why they weren't interested. Maybe we should have gone to a state senator, or to the newspapers."

In Felicidad the number of meetings with the agents increased and became more contentious.

"They began to inhabit my life morning, noon, and night, Victoria. Either they were meeting with me somewhere or in other close-by cities, calling me on the phone with more questions, or knocking on my door. I was already paranoid."

Despite her anger, Sofia was eager to learn more of what the FBI knew about her former husband's hidden agenda and how badly he had duped her but her interrogators were tight-lipped. At some of the meetings other agents joined them and she was asked to repeat much of her story, going over again and again many of the details. She was told to compose endless lists of names, dates, and places in Portland, Seattle, San Diego, La Jolla, and Mexico that she visited with her husband and friends or relatives. She was asked why she accepted so willingly Karim's excuses and explanations. Why hadn't she refused to take his non-answers when she asked him questions? She cringed at the agents' criticism and retreated into herself, refusing to answer.

In the fall of 2002 Sofia felt she was increasingly being treated as a criminal and began to omit details, hoping to end the sessions if the FBI realized they had wrung her memory dry. She was asked to stare at photos in the hope she could ID more suspects until her eyes began to blur, and she was physically and mentally exhausted. There was little compassion from her interrogators and they still spent hour after hour grilling her, making her repeat again and again detailed information and trying, she believed, to trip her up but it became too much and at times Sofia refused to answer any more questions.

"I know they needed information in order to stop another terrorist attack," Sofia said, "but I'd told them everything I knew. I needed my life back. Jarrett wasn't working and I had to get a job."

Chapter 40

Sofia's plea to be finished with her FBI interviews produced two results. She decided to get a divorce. Secondly, she cast around for employment but before she had time to check out job openings the FBI offered her temporary work. She was asked by the International FBI Unit in Sacramento to become a paid informant in Portland for two or three months.

"I told them that I wouldn't do it," she said to me. "It was more than seven or eight years since I was at our hang-outs in Portland. So much must have changed. Surely the Arabs I knew back then weren't still around. I'd imagine they all scurried back to the Middle East after 9/11 like the rats they were. But I was told that more attacks could be in the pipelines, this time on the West Coast."

When Sofia phoned Erika and told her about the FBI wanting her to pose as a tourist in Portland for a few weeks, her mother advised her to stay with it now that she had come this far.

"No, I can't do it any more, Mom. I am tense and edgy. I can't sleep and when I do drop off I have terrible nightmares."

"I know, Sofia, and I sympathize but since you are in the middle of it all, honey, you could be saving lives because of any people you might recognize still hanging around Portland. They could be looking to join a terrorist cell or are already part of a new one. You were the person who met so many of them."

"No," she told Walker on her call-back to him. "I am through. I've had enough. I need to be with my children."

During the call she realized the agent had lost none of his abrasive and suspicious attitude towards her and the thought of working for him gave her the chills. Definitely not, she told him. An hour later Sofia received a call from Special Agent Terry Johnson with the FBI's domestic terrorism unit in Portland. He offered her the same job but working for him instead of for Walker. Johnson was gentle, kind, and understanding. He said she would start receiving a salary upfront and it would be generous. Sofia, in almost dire straits financially, agreed to an initial meeting at Johnson's Portland office.

The agent turned out to be stocky, green-eyed, and well-built with a nose that appeared to have been broken once or twice. He assured Sofia that she had his respect. She took to the agent immediately and felt a rapport. Johnson explained he was taking over her case as lead agent and told her about the workings of the U.S. Government's Joint Task Force on Terrorism which included the Federal Bureau of Investigation, the Central Intelligence Agency, the National Security Agency, and others. Later it would include Homeland Security. Johnson told her that the task force admitted her suspicions were true about the so-called students plotting an attack on Portland when she was living with Karim. He gave her no details but she believed him.

"I really need your help," he said. "We're sure there are terrorist sleeper cells here in the city and you are one of the only people we know who might be able to recognize some of Karim's friends from your time with him. They'll be older, of course, but not very much changed and probably living the same lifestyle as before. As I told you earlier, we'll pay you for your time spent working for us undercover."

The promised salary was crucial. Jarrett's income from the drug trade was diminishing as he spent more and more time drinking and sleeping. The arrangement would mean leaving her two little boys with their grandmother, Sally, who adored them, but Sofia would visit every other week if possible. She would take Cody with her to Dundee and they'd both stay with Erika and Rowland until Johnson found her a place to stay in Portland.

She and Cody set off from Felicidad. After a week in Dundee her son settled in well with Erika. He was registered at the local school and basked in having a close relationship with his grandfather,

Rowland, and Erika who had helped to look after him after he was born and for months afterwards until Sofia married Jarrett and went to live in California.

Special Agent Johnson soon took her to her new accommodations, a small hotel away from downtown. Neither of them knew how long the undercover job would last but he assured her he would not overwork her. While she unpacked her suitcase he laid out what he wanted her to do, namely frequent Portland's bars, clubs, fast food and other restaurants she used to go to with Karim, as well as other venues such as the video stores and the bank although the account must have been closed years ago. Nevertheless, she and Jonson went to meet with the bank manager to check when the accounts were closed. In 2000, he told them.

Provided with a new cell phone Sofia was to call the agent if she saw anyone she knew from her previous time with Karim and tell Johnson where she was so he could join her. When she called he appeared at her side so quickly she suspected he was always following her.

As it happened, Sofia recognized two bearded Arabs at the Salonika Bar downtown. They'd been at her house frequently studying the ordnance maps or flipping through Karim's porno magazines. One of them, the shorter of the two, she only saw a couple of times, then he never returned. Maybe he had been turned down as unsuitable as a recruit for not living up to the required standard, she told the agent. This happened with only a few of the men.

The Arabs in question at the Salonika were no longer dressed as students in jeans and T-shirts but were far more formal. They reminded her of her husband, the shower hound, with their well-groomed and well-clothed appearance. They were probably only in their late 20s, the FBI agent told her, and still relevant. Sofia reflected that the passing years since she'd seen them were probably responsible for their changed appearances as they were out of college. She wondered if they had graduated, if they had jobs, and where they lived these days. She was assured that the FBI would check them out.

Sofia took Johnson to the video store that she, Karim, and their buddies frequented. Posing as a customer while the agent sat outside in the car, she recognized three Arabs, then left the store. She got back into the car and pointed them out where they were visible through the store window.

"I don't know their names but I know that cologne and body odor," she told the agent.

Johnson told her to wait in the car while he went inside. Sofia assumed he took photos with the tiny camera he held in the palm of his hand.

She also took the agent to the Middle Eastern bazaar but she failed to see anyone she knew while chatting about the sharp aroma of spices that reminded her of a specialty grocery store she also showed Johnson. A train whistle in the distance it reminded her to tell him about the photos taken of specific train tracks, and of watching the Rose Parade where the Arabs appeared to be calculating attendance numbers at the annual event, one of Portland's most famous that drew people from all over the country.

By now Johnson was able to tell Sofia that the FBI was pleased with her cooperation and with the hard facts she told them about the men's duplicitous lives. But for her part, the stress of the constant driving around to re-live her former life, which at first had been idyllic, became too much. Exhausted and still sick at heart, she wanted to be done with it. Although it was great to see her brother, Alan, again occasionally when he came to Portland on business, Sofia felt like a stranger, rootless, and alone although she made weekly trips to Erika's house to be with Cody. She needed to go home to Felicidad, too. She missed the two little boys despite the bi-weekly visits. Maybe she and Jarrett could reconcile.

How to convince Johnson and any agents who might be following her that she really needed to wrap up her cooperation? It had lasted nine months in total. She had nothing more to give. The FBI had her photos and documents. She needed to tell Johnson she was done, to let them all know she was serious.

After buying a can of black spray paint at a hardware store she drove to her hotel and parked.

She took the can from its bag, went to the back of her car, shook the can a few times, pressed the knob, and painted in big, bold letters on the outside of the rear window, "I QUIT."

It was time for her life to return to normal, whatever that was these days. She packed up, told the hotel desk she was leaving, and drove to Erika's house in Dundee. There she gathered up Cody's belongings, said goodbye to her parents, and she and her son drove east, headed for Felicidad. She apologized to Cody for taking him out of school but assured the boy he'd be able to go back to his old school and see his friends again.

As the miles passed, with Cody asleep on the back seat, she thought about the state of her current marriage. She needed to have an honest talk with Jarrett about the divorce. Maybe they should move to a big city where she could find a good job, hopefully in Northern California, perhaps in Merced, so that if there was a divorce she could satisfy the divorce requirements with regard custody of the children. Most divorces required spouses to live in the same state so that the other spouse had access to the children.

Sofia abandoned all dreams of being a fashion designer, at least for the near future. Now, all she wanted was to survive, heal, and love her three boys. She resolved to push the events of the past months out of her mind and focus on beginning a new life. It surely, she promised herself, had to be better than the one she was leaving behind.

As she crossed the state line from Oregon into Northern California she breathed a huge sigh of relief but for the first few miles she couldn't resist checking the rearview mirror in case agents were following her. The large black letters she had painted on the window were still there but didn't obstruct her ability to keep an eye on any cars that could be suspect. She saw no vehicles that appeared to be on her tail although she exited the highway a couple of times to make sure before driving back on at the next entrance. They were letting her go. At least for now.

"I couldn't blame them for their attitude towards me in the frantic days after 9/11," she said as I continued tape recording. "They needed to squeeze every drop of information from me regardless of what it took to do so. They were under tremendous pressure to understand the hijackers. I'm sure every law enforcement agency that the government threw at the task worked feverishly night and day to figure it all out. As for me, I knew that my regrets must have sounded shallow compared to the grief, shock, pain, and death that 9/11 brought to the victims."

As she re-lived the past several weeks in her mind she thought fondly of Agent Johnson, comparing his gentleness to that of the Sacramento FBI agents towards her. As she saw Felicidad loom up ahead she gave the men a pass for their ugly behavior during their meetings, excusing it as part of the panicked aftermath of 9/11. She vowed to erase them from her memory.

Cody awoke and they sang upbeat songs along with the disks Sofia played on the car's CD player. He chatted animatedly about the scenery they passed, pointing out horses and cows and identifying the crops in the fields. Sofia enjoyed listening to her child, a beacon of sanity and innocence amongst the past she'd had to dredge up for the FBI.

"Hey, Cody," she said. "Only two more miles and we'll be there."

Chapter 41

In Felicidad Sofia gloried in once more being with Benjie and Hank as their full-time mother and made it a mission to resume a relationship with Jarrett, spending the next few days living a normal family life before looking for a job. The boys were still great buddies and Cody relished his role as their protector. But despite Sofia's effort to repair her marriage the damage had been done. It was only too evident that the relationship had crumbled beyond repair. Both sides agreed to separate. Finding it difficult to live together Sofia decided to take the children back to her mother's to live in Dundee while she and Jarrett sorted out a separation agreement by telephone and custody.

However, before Sofia could leave Jarrett suddenly filed for divorce and set up dates and times for meetings with lawyers. During the first meeting she learned she would be denied custody of their two sons. It appeared that her past, as well as her previous marriage to a 9/11 hijacker and the subsequent lengthy interactions with the FBI, continued to impact her life. She was to be denied any version of joint custody and, in fact, any type of custody of Benjie and Hank. Cody, of course, was exempt. The court decision sent Sofia into a deep depression.

Erika urged her daughter to come home to Dundee for at least a week or two to get her head straight before she made any decisions about the divorce.

"At least you'll have Cody with you since he is not involved in this battle. We'll figure it out together," said Erika. "We can register him again in school here."

Sofia left Felicidad after telling the two younger sons she'd be back every other weekend and to be on their best behavior with Papa and especially with Grandma who would be looking after them again for a while. The constant moving from one place to another, the uncertainty of what her future was to be, and her current financial straits, added to Sofia's dark moods.

Once more Sofia drove to her childhood town with Cody. Looking over at him sitting quietly in the passenger seat watching the miles go by as he had before, Sofia hoped he wouldn't be too lonely. Maybe there was a summer camp he could go to although how would he feel being away from her again? No, she thought, I'll keep him with me. There must be something local, like the Boy Scouts, or summer swim school. Maybe the YMCA has a day camp.

Taking refuge with her mother and stepfather might be just what she needed at this point. It would give both her and her husband a break to consider custody, alimony, and child support, she reflected. Perhaps I can finish high school and begin a career in retailing after all. I'll need to find a job close to Felicidad so I can be near the kids. Even if I'm denied any version of live-in custody surely I will be allowed to visit with the children regularly, even for a few hours. And Cody, of course, will still be with me. The thought lifted her mood until the memory returned of her little boys' faces as they watched her pack up her and Cody's belongings and load them into the car.

Welcomed again by her mother Sofia nevertheless lapsed into despondency once more. She couldn't shake a feeling of impending doom. She felt a great hopelessness and the emotions took a toll. Erika made a huge fuss over Cody, taking him on outings by herself to shield him from his mother's moods.

After a couple of weeks Sofia settled down, came out of her melancholia, and sought a job at the dress shops where she used to be a customer. She signed up for classes in fashion design. For extra employment there were restaurants at the Dundee mall that might need her experience from her waitressing at the Angus Grill steak house. She figured she'd be able to handle a full-time as well as a part-time job on weekends.

"At the back of my mind, of course, Victoria," Erika said on the phone to me during one of our many lengthy calls, "was the question of whether the FBI was really through with me and our family. I'm sure they knew I wanted to write a book because I was taking notes like crazy at my debriefing sessions, and maybe from tapping my phone. They also must have known I wasn't about to reveal any state secrets in my book because I didn't know any."

Erika emphasized that Sofia's main reason for getting her story published was the same as her own – to warn other people who might see something, a red flag, that they thought could be terrorist-oriented, an unusual behavior, or even hear a threat against America.

"Yes, it sure is a different mindset today," I told her. "Sofia's true recounting of her experiences with the hijacker and his terrorist buddies is mind-blowing and deserves to be told."

Happily, after three months of intense work interviewing the family, visiting the locations, and driving down to Tijuana to check out the nightclubs and the system of security at the U.S.-Mexico border, I decided that I had almost all the material and information I needed to begin writing the book. The cassette tape recordings had been transcribed by a service in Los Angeles and copies made of the documents. Although there was still minor research to complete, I estimated that one more trip to Dundee to meet with Sofia a final time would wrap it up.

I was more eager to ghostwrite Sofia's book than any other memoir or autobiography I had tackled, a total of nine at that point. Some of my clients were famous, like 1930s heartthrob singer Rudy Vallee and his wife, Ellie; a few were celebrity athletes; I wrote a U.S. Ambassador's biography, a book for a nuclear physicist, and another for an oil baron.

Not all of my clients wanted their stories commercially sold to the public but written and printed privately in book form for their families and future generations to read. I knew from interviews with some young relatives they had no idea of the kind of life their ancestors may have endured or enjoyed, especially those who served in America's wars in foreign lands such as World War II, Korea, Vietnam, and the Gulf War. Most returning military veterans refused to talk about their experiences and wanted to move on. However, setting any records straight was important to them as they entered their senior years. They wanted their grandchildren to know their family heritage and history.

I planned to end Sofia's book with her and the children beginning a new life. She had taken back her maiden name of Wainwright which she had also given to Cody when filling out his birth certificate. With two marriages behind her Sofia told me she felt that using her father's name was the right thing to do. It seemed a little odd to me because her other sons bore Jarrett's name. But perhaps she felt she wanted to wipe the slate clean. Thus, the final chapter in her book, she and I agreed, would be a happy one of celebration, of life returning to a steady pace and of rearing the children in an America free of terrorist plots.

Did I believe Sofia's story? I'd developed a sort of sixth sense when sitting across from a potential client but I had been hoodwinked twice. Her sincerity, to me, rang true and my antennae never so much as quivered.

Chapter 42

While waiting in Dundee for Jarrett to tell her when to return to California one final time to sign the divorce papers and sort out different matters in person rather than by mail, Sofia began practicing her Jehovah's Witnesses religion more faithfully. Yet, although the beliefs included no celebrations of birthdays or holidays, she decided that marking Christmas with all of its festive its trimmings, the Christmas lights, tinsel, ornaments, a tree, gifts for all four of them, and a turkey dinner would give Cody a big lift. He missed his little brothers and for the first time since they were born Sofia wouldn't be spending the holiday with all three of her sons.

On the first day of December, Sofia went shopping with a light heart, buying a few toys and clothing for the children, and gifts for Erika, Rowland, and Anne who remained in San Diego with her fiancé. Sofia wrapped and mailed the gifts to Benjie and Hank. She also sent a gift to their grandma, Sally, who Sofia knew was taking great care of the boys. The rest of the gifts would be piled under the

Christmas tree, anticipating Cody's delight at passing them around to his mom and grandparents.

First, of course, they needed a tree. The house was small so Sofia knew the tree had to be under 4ft. She wanted a live tree, not one of the plastic fakes she saw in the stores. She planned to walk around the Christmas tree farm she had in mind for a while to enjoy the scent of the pine and fir trees rather than buying the first tree she considered would suit her needs.

"Mom, I'm going to that Christmas tree farm above Beaverton Creek and get us a real tree. It'll have to be small enough to fit through the Honda's hatchback or maybe the owner can tie it onto the roof for me."

"You know as Jehovah's Witnesses we don't celebrate Christmas."

"Of course I know but I just feel like doing it this year and Cody will enjoy it. It's the first time in three years he won't be with his brothers or his dad, you know. Another thing is, when Victoria comes back up here next week for a final taping for the book I'd like to welcome her with a decorated tree. I have a gift for her, too. I'm really looking forward to telling her about any holes in my story she might need to fill when she gets here."

That was true. I was ready to make one more trip to Oregon in four days' time, in early December. I needed just a few details of Sofia's experiences with Karim and then the next month, January, 2006

I could start structuring and writing the book. I was tremendously eager to begin and I was confident that the project was well in hand. I had completed so much research it occupied three large plastic storage bins. Each file, and there were 102 of them, bulged with background on each member of Sofia's family, the homes she lived in with Karim in Portland and San Diego, the McDonald's where Anne worked, the cars the Arabs leased and drove, the dozens of transcribed cassette tapes, and a myriad other pieces of information necessary to the writing of her book.

Sofia had been very forthcoming about her emotions throughout our taping sessions, laying bare the passion she'd once felt for Karim, the heartaches, the disappointments, and the joys of her teenage years. In retrospect I had to keep reminding myself that she was only 19 when she had gone through a marriage and a divorce. At 21 years old she had a son with no support from his father. Her experiences with the FBI, which at times were harrowing and debilitating to her mental and physical health, took place in her late 20s.

My main concern was to ensure that her story came across as truthful and sincere. Certainly, the documents backed up everything she told me, as did the names of the FBI agents both in Fresno and Portland, in addition to the family's own recollections.

I'd asked Sofia if she wanted me to structure the book as a memoir, a biography, or an autobiography.

261

After I explained the differences she chose biography. I enjoyed writing non-fiction, although I also wrote fiction. I found people's real lives as fascinating as any fabricated characters. I knew that this project was going to be both a challenge and a joy, an opportunity for Sofia to put to bed her negative experiences and memories. Sometimes, when dredging up some of the bad times, my clients found it difficult to relive them, but I hoped they served as catharsis.

Sofia's book would give readers the glimpse under the radar of a hijacker's home life in this country, of his day-to-day activities with his "friends" and "relatives," and what they were really like under the skin aside from the anti-American and al Qaeda propaganda they spouted.

I planned to point out Karim's habits and customs that affected his relationship with Sofia. A few of the files I had accumulated covered details such as the clothing and headdresses Arabs wore, their culture and cuisine, information about their countries, their attitudes towards America, and other relevant data. I had voluminous folders containing Sofia's own journals, the margins covered in abstract doodles that appeared to have no meaning except for heart-shaped drawings on some of the pages, all in thick black marker that brought back memories of her description of the pen bugs placed in her car by the agents. Who else would have been responsible?

My smallest storage bin held the 9/11 Commission Report and the several other books I'd bought to read. I was astounded at the smallest details the authors discovered and wrote about in such a short time after the attacks. I was struck, too, by the warnings and red flags years earlier that the U.S. government itself missed or failed to comprehend. I also had piles of newspaper clippings, magazine articles, and a few videos. Most precious were the copies of Sofia's documents and other material.

With a plethora of research materials and taped interviews, with a final meeting on the calendar, I was sure I had sufficient information to write the book that Sofia had set her heart on publishing. On my next and probably final trip to meet with Sofia before starting to write, she'd said she would give me the last of the copies of her notes. She'd told me they weren't that important but she wanted me to have them anyway in case there was a nugget in there worth unearthing. As a ghostwriter I often saw value in materials that clients dismissed as uninteresting until I pointed out their relevance.

I had already decided that my final session with Sofia would focus on how she would like to end the book. It would be a happy, upbeat ending now that she had unburdened herself to me of the experiences of those dark days. She'd re-lived her teenage marriage and the divorce with tears, recriminations, and a few laughs as I tape-recorded her, and she moved into happier days with Jarrett and her children. Until 9/11 and the FBI took over her life. Now, with our final meeting and her re-telling of her story all behind her, I looked forward to seeing that sunny, radiant smile again.

She was, I think, more excited than I was that she would bring her intent into reality and finally be free of any lingering demons. I asked if she would agree to a publicity tour later on, and she was reluctant at first but then she realized how necessary it would be to do so in order to have her story believed and accepted. Her appearances on national and probably international television would be an important part of the success of the project.

Throughout the relating of her life with Karim and its aftermath Sofia told me she still suffered occasional bouts of depression. I hoped that telling me her story for future publication would help relieve them. Thankfully, the paranoia that had occasionally invaded her mind no longer bothered her after her involvement with the FBI came to an end.

She gave me additional copies of her marriage certificate and divorce decree, photos, excerpts from her secret journals detailing her debriefings, and other material. I wondered at so many duplicate copies and if she feared I'd lose them or they'd be confiscated. I know that an FBI file existed on myself as a reporter when I covered the Black Panthers and Mafia trials on the East Coast.

When Sofia suggested I should keep the copies in a safe place I could see she was still nervous about the entire project. Although her family had come around to accepting the fact that her life and theirs would become public and embarrass them, they understood her reasoning for coming forward as soon as her meetings with law enforcement ended and she was able to resume her life. Was she brave and courageous for sharing what she knew about her hijacker husband a couple of weeks after 9/11? There was certainly still panic and consternation from the White House on down with the U.S. government scrambling to explain the attacks and discover and contain future plots.

For my part I was hoping that Sofia's revelations in her book would be well-received considering the huge amount of detail and confirmation I had amassed including her tape recordings, along with the tapes of her mother, two sisters, and two brothers. My fervent wish and hope was that Sofia would no longer be a target on anyone's radar.

It was to become a wish unfulfilled.

Chapter 43

"You're going to Beaverton Creek for a Christmas tree? That's thirty-five miles away," said Erika as she, Rowland, Sofia, and Cody ate breakfast. "Could be icy up there. Why not go to the Christmas tree lot next to the mall?"

"Those trees are too expensive, Mom. Besides, I want to show Cody how beautiful the view is from the mountain."

"No, Mom, I don't want to go," said her son. "I can't go. Sammy is coming over and we're going to make s'mores at Chuck's house. His dad's going to build a bonfire in their backyard. It'll be real fun. Please let me go."

Sofia, in a pensive mood, nodded her agreement to Cody's plan, seeing his eyes light up at the prospect of the camp-like outing. She helped Erika clear the table and wash the dishes, then put on her puffy red ski jacket. She told her mother she was kind of glad to have a little time alone, especially on the mountain which she hadn't visited since grade school.

It was just after 9 a.m. on December 3, 2005 when Sofia set off in her little Honda Accord. She kissed Cody goodbye, waved to Erika already at her sewing machine, and left. Three or four inches of snow lay on the ground, a familiar winter scene in Dundee. On the backseat of the Honda were two boxes of her secret journals and copious notes of her meetings with the FBI agents. In the margins of the pages were large abstract doodles that appeared to mean nothing. There were also cryptic notes written in her signature block letters in thick black ink. Sofia kept her files with her at all times, lugging them into her mother house each night, and back into the car in the morning if she was driving somewhere, laying them on floor of the back seat hidden under a couple of old towels.

As Sofia drove towards her destination, smiling to a neighbor as she passed him, she began to think of her current situation and how thrilled she was to be rid of the FBI, their questions, their obvious distrust of her, and her memories of Karim. A new life beckoned despite the divorce from Jarrett. The teacher of her night classes in fashion design was more and more complimentary of her illustrations and told her she was her most talented student. Sofia gave a mental nod of thanks to Erika whose dressmaking skills everyone knew were superb. Next year, Sofia thought, maybe I can get a job as an assistant with the Kate Donovan House of Design.

My portfolio is already filled with ideas and I've been careful to render the sketches as meticulously as any Paris couturier.

Happy to be buying a Christmas tree, her first one as a single parent, she took a left turn onto the steep, snow-covered turnoff for Black Saddle Mountain. A couple of cars were coming down with fir trees strapped to their roofs. Close behind her was a large, black SUV. The driver seemed to be in a hurry because he was right on her tail. She looked for a widening in the narrow, winding off-road mountain trail to pull over and allow him to pass. Two miles up she saw a spot on the left-hand side, opposite to the mountain edge, and parked but the driver didn't take up the offer. He stayed right behind her. Maybe there's not enough room, she thought, for him to pass.

A little farther on, within fifty feet or so, she came upon another widening in the trail, this time on the right hand side. It overlooked a deep gorge where the turbulent creek flowed swiftly 200 feet below, swollen with melted snow. She stopped there and decided to drink the coffee she'd brought along and enjoy the spectacular view while she let the SUV go by. She picked up the coffee cup from the center console next to her seat, took a sip, and almost dropped the cup as she thought: What's that jolt I just felt?

Chapter 44

It took three and a half hours before Sofia's body was freed from the half-submerged Honda that ended upside-down, its front end and right side crushed, in the rushing frigid waters of the creek. The length of time it took the Dundee County sheriff's department and rescuers caused her family to believe she might have died of hypothermia trapped inside the car as it was buffeted by the swirling river. The official report stated that it had plunged off the cliff, apparently deliberately by the action of the driver, according to two witnesses. One of the witnesses said he saw movement down below when he got out of his SUV to peer over the edge high above and saw an arm half-outside the rolled-down driver-side window. When Sofia was finally removed from the car much later it was determined she was dead.

A tow truck was called but the towing company was alleged to have been reluctant to come out, although they later did so. A Search and Rescue Team was also called to the scene because the area was said to be extremely difficult to access and required rescuers to use ropes to climb down the cliff.

The accident was under investigation for more than two weeks. Finally, it was determined to be "non-criminal" and the official cause of death was "Suicide." Did Sofia really commit suicide? Did her guilt of being a terrorist bride finally overwhelm her? Or was her car deliberately pushed off the cliff? If so, by whom? Another possibility was that if she thought she was being followed and, scared, blindly accelerated did she herself send her car accidentally over the edge? Perhaps the crash was perpetrated by one side or the other, the good guys or the bad guys. It was possible that neither group wanted her full story to be told and presented to the public.

Was the FBI covering up because of lax visa enforcement back then or embarrassment at ignoring Sofia's previous warnings, or did al Qaeda want her dead in revenge for identifying terrorists in Portland, as well as needing to protect their operatives currently living in the U.S. and still plotting against the country?

Many of these questions were never answered to the satisfaction of Erika and her family members, especially not for Ben who worked as a manager and chief mechanic at an auto dealership. When he visited the scene of his sister's death plunge over the edge of the mountain road early the next morning before the sheriffs arrived to inspect the scene he studied the Honda's tire marks. They were still evident in the snow and he was immediately struck by their direction. They didn't seem right to him. He had read the police report and there appeared to be contradictions. The tire tracks were not in the direction that a front-wheel drive car would spin if the car was pointed towards the edge of the cliff. It was all wrong, he thought.

"The report stated there were witnesses that saw her car go off the cliff." Ben said. "At that point of the narrow road there are two bends with no room for more than one car right there and you can't see around the turns. There's a hill you go up so if her car slid she'd never have plunged into the gorge. She was said to be at the only place where you can do a three-point turn but it was way up around the two bends in the road so it didn't make sense to me that the witnesses said they had seen her drive off the cliff."

I heard the frustration in Ben's voice as he further explained his reasoning.

"From where a witness said he was behind the Honda there's also a huge rock that blocks the view. There was no way he or anyone else could have seen her accelerate, as claimed, and watch her go over the edge. I've gone up to that spot four times and you simply cannot see a car at that spot, or what she did, from another car because as I said there's no room for more than one car. Another witness said she was holding a cup of coffee and looked like a deer in the headlights. But if she had turned her car to face outwards towards the gorge how could they see her eyes which would be away from them?"

When Ben attempted to find out the truth he claimed that law enforcement officials refused to talk to him. He tried to contact one of the two witnesses to the fatal event, whom he discovered to be a retired FBI agent with no address available, without success. Again, he hit a brick wall. His efforts proved futile. The Coroner's toxicology report stated there were no drugs, legal or otherwise, in Sofia's system. She was found to be in good health and free of any health issues. The family wondered why no autopsy was performed on her body as required in what the Wainwrights considered a questionable cause of death.

Ben also pointed out that one reason it took three and a half hours to free her was in part, he was told, because she was held in by her seatbelt. However, a U.S. forestry officer said that she was not strapped in. Another point Ben made was that the report stated it took so long to access her because the terrain was difficult but the tow truck operator, when he finally arrived, told Ben it only took ten minutes to walk in his waders, get to Sofia's car, and hook it up for towing.

"The timeline of reaching the Honda was suspect," Sofia's brother maintained, "because the sheriff's office was only eleven miles from the accident site. Yet they said it took them two hours to reach her. The witnesses said she went over around

11 a.m. No one even started getting to the car until 1 p.m. and although the spot may have been difficult to reach there were too many conflicting stories. I came to the conclusion that my sister did not commit suicide as claimed. The reports just didn't match up."

Was it possible that another car or a pickup truck was coming from the opposite direction and maybe got too close on the narrow mountain path, accidentally forcing her off the cliff? Or was someone really trying to silence her? Sadly, these questions would never be answered to the family's satisfaction. Speculation was all they were left with.

Authorities said they found several pieces of paper floating in the water downstream, including a few pages from her secret journals, which were dried and then handed over to Erika. None of the boxes of notes she always kept in the car or in Erika's house were recovered or seen anywhere in the creek. Neither were they found at Erika's home when she searched for them. Luckily, perhaps with prescience, Sofia had already passed along to me copies of her files during my several trips to Dundee.

Chapter 45

I had just stepped out of the shower when the phone rang. It was Erika. I figured she wanted to confirm the date of my visit and probable arrival at her house. I knew she had several dressmaking jobs she was working on and needed to schedule her time with me.

"Hi, Erika, good to hear your voice. I'm looking forward to seeing you and Sofia again later this week."

"I hope you are sitting down, Victoria. I have some terrible news."

"What is it?"

"Sofia's car went off a cliff and she was killed. You had best cancel any plans for coming up here."

At that point Erika broke down, said she'd call me again soon, and we both hung up.

Stunned, I couldn't imagine how anything like that could have happened. Last time I talked to Sofia she was looking forward to our wrap-up session although she did sound a little down.

Killed?

I was immediately suspicious because we both knew Sofia was taking a risk wanting to publish a book about her experiences with Karim as one of the 9/11 hijackers. She had recounted to me every detail she could remember of their time together, the "student" gatherings at their homes in Portland and San Diego, the Arabs that Sofia met, her ex-husband's brothers and cousins if that's what they really were, the trips to La Jolla and Mexico, and the details of her debriefings by the FBI. Sofia told me of Karim's mysterious meetings, whispered conversations, and her suspicions that he was having an affair. In that respect she was correct to be suspicious but for an entirely different reason. There was A Big Wedding, the codename for 9/11, as Hicks' book revealed, but not the one Sofia envisioned. Was she the target of the bad guys or the good guys? Had she become a loose cannon to the FBI or to the al Qaeda terrorists? Had those she'd pointed out to law enforcement agents during her "tourist" visits to bars and restaurants in Portland taken revenge?

Perhaps I had misunderstood Erika's words about Sofia's car going off a cliff. I realized as I played back the call in my mind Erika had not given me any specific reason for Sofia's sudden death. Was it accidental, deliberate, a suicide? I checked out the local Dundee newspaper for reports of the accident, if that is what it was, and waited for Erika to call me back.

In the meantime I sorted through the bins that held my cassettes, the transcriptions, Sofia's notes and documents, and the mounds of research although I was unsure if I would ever put them to any use. Perhaps Erika will cancel the entire project, I thought, or, like Sofia, would want the truth to be told. The decision rested on Erika's shoulders.

Three weeks later I drove up to Dundee with a heavy heart. I knew seeing the family again would be difficult. As proved to be the case. This time I stayed at a motel closer to Erika, Rowland, and Cody, and met with Jeff and Anne, who came up from San Diego for the funeral, and stayed on for a while. Alan and Ben drove to Dundee to meet with me, and poured their hearts out, with Ben more voluble than the others. He was convinced that his sister was deliberately targeted and killed although it was unclear which side may have decided to do the deed. Was it a 9/11 victim's family member?

During my drive to north I was reminded of the Karen Silkwood case. The similarities between the two women were striking. Both died in questionable car crashes. Both were mothers of three children, divorced, and were killed in their small Hondas. Silkwood had expressed her concerns about the nuclear plant where she worked during her testimony before the U.S. Atomic Energy Commission. Deciding to go public with her evidence after authorities refused to take her seriously – like Sofia

– Karen had agreed to meet with a New York Times reporter with a view to getting the truth out and publicizing her story. Again, similar to Sofia's intention.

On her way to the meeting, according to theories proposed by several investigative journalists, Silkwood's car was rear-ended or pushed from behind. Once again, was it similar to Sofia's cause of death? Law enforcement claimed Karen Silkwood had simply had a fatal car accident. She was 28 years old when she somehow went off the road and crashed into a culvert. Sofia was 31 when she went off the cliff.

While the Sofia Wainwright death was ruled non-criminal and a suicide, her family pointed out there were discrepancies between the Coroner's, the sheriff's, and eye witness reports, raising suspicions among Sofia's siblings. Was Sofia's death an accident, a suicide, or was she deliberately forced off the road similar to questions surrounding the Karen Silkwood case years earlier? Erika never received a definitive answer about her daughter's death.

"Victoria, my highest priority," Sofia said the last time she and I met in Dundee for a recording session, "was to assist the FBI despite some of my family begging me to stay silent."

When I'd called Erika back, having absorbed with sorrow the almost-unbelievable news of Sofia's sudden and shocking death, she ended our call with the reminder that, above all, her daughter had made a noble decision by going to the FBI and working with them despite the potential for personal danger.

"Sofia was motivated by the belief," said Erika, "that the 9/11 victims' families were entitled to know facts about the hijackers' lives that they would never read in the newspapers. There were details of a more personal nature of those murderous terrorists that Sofia knew that should be shared with the authorities."

Certainly, the Commission Report, written by an independent, bi-partisan panel, faulted the U.S. Government's own civilian defense services in a chapter on foresight and hindsight. There was much criticism cited of non-cooperation and non–communication between U.S. law enforcement agencies, each jealously guarding their territory.

Unlike the attack on Pearl Harbor that was perpetrated by the Japan Air Force, the 9/11 event was planned and undertaken by a group of civilians whom McDermott describes as "pilgrims, soldiers of God" in his book, "Perfect Soldiers," and who operated under the al Qaeda banner with what one reporter called trivial resources, although taking possession of America's multi-million dollar commercial planes to wreak their deadly havoc was hardly trivial. MacDermott's meticulously researched book exposed the Muslim zealots' lives and who they were, sending chills down the reader's spine. He explained why they attacked America both at home and abroad, providing warnings, although Sofia knew that hindsight in her case was useless and hopeless.

Reaching back to the context of the 1990s, the time frame of Sofia's marriage to Karim when the U.S. was the pre-eminent global military power, the Commission Report speculated on whether the leaders of America truly understood the gravity of the threat that Osama bin Laden and al Qaeda posed. Was any or sufficient evidence presented to the President and Congress leading up to 9/11?

"Neither in 2000 nor in the first eight months of 2001 did any polling organization in the United States think the subject of terrorism [was] sufficiently on the minds of the public," reads the Report, "to warrant asking a question about it in a major national survey."

For her part, Sofia planned the book to urge and encourage others to come forward if they found themselves in similar circumstances, not only by contacting and working with the FBI and other U.S. agencies who now appear ready to listen, but also how to spot red flags and suspicious situations She hoped that by writing her book it could help to relieve and absolve herself of the shame and humiliation after her private life was exposed. She also wanted not only skeptical strangers and the public to grasp the implications of her story but also her three children when they were old enough to understand.

"It is my daughter Sofia's legacy," said Erika. "The family is proud of her for coming forward despite the danger we warned her of, and providing authorities with information. She was a courageous woman."

As the Wainwright family slipped back into anonymity I filed away the photos, the documents, the divorce decree, the death certificate, and the coroner's report along with the dozens of tape recordings that I had amassed, and Sofia's photo.

Perhaps one day, I thought, with a contract already signed with Erika giving me the rights to all of her daughter's journals and notes, I would complete the circle and write the memoir that Sofia herself wanted so eagerly and passionately to share. One day, perhaps.

Made in the USA
Las Vegas, NV
21 December 2021

39109504R00169